the women of hearts book six

MARCI BOLDEN

RUNAWAY HEARTS

ISBN-13: 978-1-950348-76-3

the women of hearts book six

MARCI BOLDEN

RUNAWAY HEARTS

PINK SAND
PRESS

PROLOGUE

December 8, 1989...

Annette Carlton sat taller and held her breath. After several seconds of not hearing anything other than the television, she fumbled with the remote and muted the sound. With her ears perked, she again stopped breathing and focused.

Something had bumped in the kitchen. Something that sounded too loud to be the cat. Even so, she hesitantly called out, "Oliver?"

The cat didn't respond. Not that he ever had.

There were independent felines, and then there was her orange tabby. The only time she saw the ball of fur was when his bowl was empty. Or when he started crying out for no apparent reason in the middle of the night. She suspected that was simply to annoy her because whenever she would roll herself out of bed to investigate, she never found anything other than her dumb cat sitting in the dark screaming to himself.

Several more seconds passed with no sound coming from the kitchen. Finally, Annette turned the sound back on and settled into her sofa to watch her favorite show. Her evening routine was always the same. Home by five thirty, dinner in front of the television while she watched the news, then she'd clean up her mess and curl up on the sofa to watch the VHS recordings of her soap opera. Once that was done, she showered and took a book to bed. Lights out by nine so she could get up and do it all over again.

Some people might have found her life boring, but Annette liked the comfort of every day being the same. She didn't like surprises or spontaneity. She'd had enough of that when she was younger and had to constantly guess which utility would get turned off and where her next meal would come from. Her dad had been worthless, and her mom had gotten tired of him and left. Too bad she hadn't taken Annette with her.

Now that she was grown and on her own, Annette found comfort in the routine she'd created. Knowing she had a job to go to five days a week gave her security for the first time in her life. Not only did she have the ability and willingness to pay her bills, but she always had food in the fridge. And she even had a cat who wanted nothing to do with her.

As Annette watched the couple on her screen move in for their first kiss, Oliver let out a low meow and then darted out of the kitchen.

Gasping, Annette sat straight up.

Her heart pounded hard as she watched her cat race toward the back of the house.

"What has gotten into you?" she muttered. As soon as

the cat disappeared, she eased back and focused on the television again. Though her heart was racing, she did her best to relax and enjoy her show. She was almost able to breathe normally again when she sensed she was being watched.

Her breath caught in her throat as she slowly turned her eyes toward the kitchen where Oliver had screamed and run from.

There, a man, at least six feet tall, stood. A malevolent smile curved his lips as she took him in from his boots to the dagger tattoo covering his right forearm to his bald head.

"I've been waiting for you," he said in what sounded like a New England accent... Boston, maybe.

Annette sat frozen until he pulled a knife from behind his back.

Screaming, she jumped to her feet and ran toward the front door.

She didn't make it.

[1]

Present day...

Estrada Investigations was like HEARTS Investigative Services. Except...not quite.

E.I. reeked of testosterone and moderately priced cologne. The cases weren't nearly as interesting, and the investigators weren't nearly as quick to jump in on topics like Hollywood breakups, the best mascara, or the latest fashion.

Even so, Samantha Turner was determined to make the most of her new position as a cyber investigator at E.I. Victor Estrada was giving her an amazing opportunity, and she wasn't going to blow it—despite her history of blowing things. Her latest blow job, as she liked to call her missteps in life, was pissing her former boss off so much that she had to find new employment.

Sam never thought she'd leave her job as the computer guru and ultimate research nerd for HEARTS. She'd loved working with the all-female team of private investigators.

They had gone from coworkers to friends to basically being sisters. However, nothing Sam ever did seemed to make her boss happy. *Former* boss.

Sam was far too light and airy for Holly's deep, dark, soulless outlook on life. They didn't have the same taste in men, clothes, or jokes. Holly actually didn't have any taste for jokes. She was about as amused by Sam as a bear in shackles. Sam had worked around that for as long as she could.

However, when Holly announced her engagement, Sam had forgotten just how oil-and-water their relationship could be. She was desperate to help Holly have an amazing wedding. And that had been the beginning of the end.

Holly had never been known for having a soft side, but Sam finally got fed up with Holly's blatant disrespect for her and her work and quit during one of their heated confrontations.

Though Sam was heartbroken to leave her coworkers, within days of leaving that job, she landed on her feet at Estrada Investigations. Despite pleas from her former teammates to make amends with Holly and return to HEARTS, Sam no longer felt she belonged on their team.

And she was confident she had found her dream job as a cyber investigator. Holly would have *never* given her that kind of responsibility. And Sam was excited to have an opportunity to prove herself—mostly as a *told you so* to Holly.

Rolling her shoulders back, Sam pushed thoughts of her old job from her mind and held her head high as she walked into Estrada Investigations. While she had loved her job at HEARTS, this was the first job where she was an equal.

Of sorts.

Victor's younger brother, Javier, and their friend and fellow investigator Conner O'Riley were definitely higher on the food chain than their latest addition, but Sam was definitely more than the go-to gofer that she'd been at her last job.

Even though the atmosphere wasn't quite the same at E.I., and she had to keep more of her sarcastic comments to herself than she liked, she enjoyed the job. She enjoyed being valued for what she brought to the table. Sure, she'd only been with E.I. for like a week and still didn't have her first real case, but she still felt more valued. She still felt like part of the team.

"Good morning," she said to Lorraine, the woman who occupied the reception desk.

Sam made it a point to be extra nice to Lorraine because she, herself, had spent far too much of her time at HEARTS being overlooked by clients because she was "just the receptionist." She wanted to make doubly sure that Lorraine knew she and her hard work were appreciated. But also because Lorraine was so maternal and kind, there was no other way to respond to her.

The older woman smiled warmly. "There are donuts in the conference room for the meeting this morning."

Sam perked up. Though she tried to keep her diet on the healthier side of the line, there was no better way to start the day than a sweet pastry and a large cup of coffee.

"Oh, what's the special occasion?"

Lorraine grinned and winked. "Victor's been in an unusually good mood lately. He brought them in."

While Sam and Victor Estrada had never been anything but professional in their ten or so days of knowing each other, there was an undercurrent of something going on there. When she'd walked into E.I. for her interview with her heart racing from anxiety, the last thing she'd expected was to walk out with her heart racing because she was in lust. She could barely remember a thing about her interview.

She remembered Lorraine had walked her into the conference room. She remembered shaking three men's hands, but she only remembered looking at Victor. In fact, she had left the interview and gone straight to the closest ice cream shop to console herself because she was certain staring at the man who owned the company like he was a scoop of butter pecan was not the best way to get a job.

However, the man in question had called her the next day to offer her the job. Even better, he had asked her to start as soon as possible.

Ever since her first day, Sam had had an awfully hard time tearing her gaze away from his almost-black eyes, tanned skin, and the way his muscles rippled beneath his designer shirts.

Feeling warmth rush to her cheeks as she thought of the man who had apparently brought in donuts, she gave her head a hard shake. She was not going to get involved with her boss. Doing so would just prove Holly right. Holly had continually insisted that Sam would never be an investigator because she refused to take the work seriously. She refused to put the case above whatever else came along.

Despite what Holly might have thought, private investigators didn't have to be sticks in the damn mud. They could have lives, and even enjoy them. But Sam was not going to jump into bed with her new boss and prove a point Holly was likely sitting back and waiting on—that Sam would fail without Holly there to save her.

Unfortunately, though, the electricity that sparked between Sam and Victor whenever they were in the same room was already causing her problems. Their coworkers had picked up on the undeniable attraction between them, and while Lorraine seemed pleased, Conner and Javier gave Sam the same frowns and disapproving looks she used to get from her former boss.

So, no, Sam would not act on her attraction to Victor. No, she would not trip and fall. And, hell no, she would not screw up this new job over a man.

Nope. Not going to happen.

"Maybe he got a puppy or something," Sam said before walking away, doing what she could to dismiss the notion that his good mood had anything to do with her.

"Or something," Lorraine called after her.

Sam walked into her office—*her* office—and placed her bag on her desk. This was the first time she had a space to call her own. The reception desk at HEARTS had simply been a spot for her to sit. That hadn't been her space. She couldn't keep photos or other personal items there. Holly was far too paranoid. She'd said that by putting out personal information, even a photograph, Sam was making herself vulnerable to the people who came and went. While most of those people were clients, Holly's ability to trust them was limited. Her ability to trust *anyone* was limited.

Sam had attempted to sneak some personal items into the

area, but unfortunately for her, several of her other coworkers had agreed with Holly. Her workspace had been sterile because the women that she'd worked with were convinced someone, somewhere, someday was going to get fixated on their receptionist and stalk her or something.

However, this was *her* office. *Her* space.

She smiled as she ran her fingers over the framed photo of her and Tika that she'd put on her desk her first day at E.I. Tika was her closest friend. She was also an investigator at HEARTS. Of all of Sam's former coworkers, it was Tika who had begged Sam to make amends with Holly the most. The day Sam had stormed out of the HEARTS office, swearing she'd never go back, Tika had shown up at Sam's place with a bottle of wine, a pint of ice cream, and sad eyes.

They'd both cried, but Sam was determined that she'd done the right thing. Unless Holly apologized for being so harsh, Sam wouldn't go back. So far, Holly hadn't apologized, and Sam hadn't gone back. Now she had a new job that she was confident would be the perfect fit for her.

"Good morning," Victor said from the doorway.

Sam smiled as she met his gaze.

He didn't bother being casual about skimming over her suit. "You look nice today."

"As do you."

He smiled and winked. "Meeting starts in five. Better grab a donut and fill your mug before the guys get in there."

Then he was gone.

Just like at HEARTS, the team members at Estrada had a morning meeting every day to catch up. Unlike HEARTS, this team wasn't all women. Actually, Sam was the only female investigator at the moment. Victor handled cold cases. He enjoyed trying to solve puzzles that no one else could. Jordan worked pretty much whatever came his way. And Sam was their new cyber investigator.

Tika used to say that Sam could find anything ever looked at on the Internet. That was only a slight exaggeration. Sam knew how to find things. How to get into places where she shouldn't be, and how to do so without being detected.

Holly hadn't always appreciated Sam's abilities, but she suspected her new team would—once they decided to give her a chance. Unfortunately for Sam, she had a way of shooting herself in the foot, and that happened on the first day of her new position when it became obvious there was an attraction between her and her new boss.

Victor clearly didn't have a problem blurring the lines, but Sam was trying to do the right thing, damn it. This was her fresh start. Her chance to prove herself. And she feared she was already fumbling it. But she never had been very good at doing the right thing—at least not for herself.

"Focus," she muttered quietly when she was alone. She was a week into this job. Today might be the day. She might get her first case. Once she did, she was going to be nose to the damn grindstone. Laser focused. Singularly orientated. Nothing...and she meant *absolutely nothing*...was going to distract her.

Especially a man.

Determined to stand by her convictions, Sam walked into the conference room with her notebook in hand and went right to the snack table. She filled a cup with hot coffee, snagged a Long John, and took a seat as far from that tall drink of temptation as she could get. Which, unfortunately, wasn't nearly far enough. She was still tempted to crawl across the table and curl up in his lap.

Shit.

VICTOR COULDN'T REMEMBER THE LAST TIME HE'D HAD such a hard time focusing around a woman, but damn if Samantha Turner hadn't turned his world upside down the day she'd walked in for an interview. Though Javier and Conner had sat in the interview with him, he hadn't given them a chance to speak. He'd known he'd hire that woman as soon as she'd shaken his hand—qualifications be damned. Something about her made him want her there, with him, even if she hadn't been worth hiring.

Which he'd decided she hadn't been after reading her résumé again after she'd accepted the job.

His teammates had given him hell for hiring her based on her looks, but he was the boss. Or so he'd reminded them. He'd be concerned about sexual harassment just from the way he looked at her if she weren't looking at him the same way. She wanted him just as much and was just as open about it, and that had thrown him for a loop. She didn't seem interested in playing games or teasing.

He wasn't sure exactly what she was interested in, but he was eager to find out.

He drew a breath, about to ask her how her time at E.I.

was going. He hated small talk, but he guessed anything else between them could lead them astray rather quickly.

However, before he could ask, Conner and Javier walked in chatting about the bets they'd put on an upcoming basketball game. As his younger brother, Javier had similar features to Victor—dark hair and eyes, tan skin, and a muscular build.

Conner, however, was a thin, pale twig that came from a long line of Irishmen. Though he didn't seem to have an ounce of muscle on him, he was proficient in martial arts and could probably take down both Victor and Javier without breaking a sweat. As mild-tempered as he was most of the time, if he got fired up, their teammate could be quite fearsome. Of course, he usually only got fired up watching basketball and losing a bet to Javier.

Their chatter didn't stop until they sat at the table. Meetings were fairly casual at E.I., so Javier jumped right in without being told or asked to do so.

"Jasmine Milder was right. Her husband is a lying, cheating sleaze." He tossed a few photos from his file onto the table. "Raise your hands if you're surprised." He laughed when nobody implied they were shocked at his discovery. "I sent the photos, a write-up, and an invoice to her this morning."

"And Sarah Blackheart's case?" Victor asked as he glanced over the list of cases they were each working on.

"Nothing yet, but I'm on it," Javier said.

"Oh," Sam said as she opened a file. She slid a few pages to Javier. "Here are her husband's phone records. I emailed a digital copy to you last night."

"Awesome," he said, accepting the papers. He gave her a

weak salute. "Thank you for making my life a million times easier."

Something twinged in Victor's chest. Not jealousy, but he didn't like it. Maybe because Javier was using Sam's skills without conferring with Victor first. But that was foolish. The team always helped each other out. Rather than digging too deep into why he didn't want Sam helping Javier, Victor looked at Conner.

"And you?"

"I'm this close to proving Jared Macaulay is faking his back injury. It won't be long. He had some landscaping timbers delivered yesterday. I have no doubt he'll be out there moving those around. One good photo and it's over."

Victor nodded. He was always amazed at how easy it was to catch people scamming insurance companies.

"I found a new case to dig into," Victor said. "A murder from 1989."

He preferred cold cases. He liked digging into the past and solving things that no one else could. Times had changed, techniques had improved, and very few had time to revisit cold cases when there were so many new problems in the world. So Victor made cold cases his priority. Not to mention that older cases tended to come with a decent reward that kept their budget in a much better place than cheating spouses and fake injuries.

This particular case had a twenty-thousand-dollar reward put up by the victim's neighborhood watch, and it was still available for anyone with information that could solve the case. Victor wouldn't mind earning that reward and giving everyone at E.I. a nice holiday bonus.

"This case was particularly chilling," he said. "Annette Carlton, a young woman, was raped and murdered—stabbed to death, to be specific—in her own home. No witnesses. No evidence. However, there is DNA on file to compare to anyone who might be arrested. Apparently, he didn't bother protecting himself before having his way with her."

As soon as he'd disclosed that information, Sam sat taller, creased her brow, and tilted her head. Her interest had been piqued. She blinked those big blue eyes and leaned forward ever so slightly. "Were...were there any suspects?" she asked. "Anyone arrested?"

"Not a suspect as much as someone of interest," Victor said hesitantly. She was far too interested. Not curious, but genuinely interested, as if she had an investment in his response. "A neighbor saw a man walking down the street that she'd never seen before. Tall, bald. Wearing an oversized jacket and black boots. That wasn't enough for the police to find the man."

Curiosity filled Victor as Sam's eyes swam. Telltale signs she was trying to put her thoughts together. Something about what he'd said had sparked something in her mind.

"Are you familiar with this case?" he asked.

She blinked, sat back, and guarded herself quickly. "No."

He wasn't sure he believed that. He glanced at Javier and Conner. They didn't seem to either. Instead of pressing in front of the other investigators, Victor closed his file without disclosing more information.

Until she was honest with him, he decided he'd better keep the details a bit closer to his chest. He wasn't sure why she wouldn't come clean, but she clearly wasn't. Something about Annette Carlton's murder had rung a bell in Sam's mind.

Pulling the file closer to him, Victor glanced at his other teammates.

"Don't worry," he said to Sam. "We're going to get you a case soon. We all appreciate you jumping in and helping with the piles on our desks. You'll have your own case soon."

She blinked a few times and forced a smile to her lips. "Oh, I'm not worried. I don't mind helping where I can."

Again, her eyes moved to his file. Yeah. She was definitely interested in that case for some reason. A reason he was going to get out of her one way or another.

"Anybody have anything else?" he asked.

"Nope," Conner said.

"Nada," Javier muttered as he stood. Without another look to anyone else, he walked out with Conner on his heels.

They were barely out of the room before their taunting and teasing about the upcoming game started again. They were nearly impossible to tolerate when their favorite teams were going head-to-head, but they had been friends for years, so Victor was used to it.

He had intended to tell Sam to do her best to ignore them, but her interest in the cold case was far too distracting. He didn't care if she was put off by the childish bickering of their teammates. He cared about why she cared so much about Annette Carlton.

Victor waited until the conference room emptied. As soon as Sam rounded the round oak table, Victor stepped in the doorway, stopping her before she could leave.

She cocked one eyebrow at him and batted her false lashes.

"Don't do that," Victor said despite his amusement at her innocent act.

"What?"

"Make me ask the obvious."

Her luscious lips twitched. "I already told you I'm single."

"For which I'm eternally grateful. But that's not what I mean."

"What do you mean?" she asked in her sultry tone.

"You nearly jumped out of your seat when I started talking about that case. Why is that?"

The pull of her lips turned into a sweet but fake smile. "Sounds intriguing."

"Intriguing?"

"Yeah. I thought maybe I could help. You know, look at old jail photos and things like that. Maybe I can see if your tall, bald, boot-wearing man has ever been arrested."

Victor clearly heard the lie in her words. "You think you're going to find a suspect based on him being tall and bald?"

"And in the area where the murder took place. Where was that again?"

He drew a breath and rolled his shoulders back, losing some of his patience. Cute as he found this woman, he wasn't keen on being lied to.

"Not too far from here."

"So," she said with a shrug, "I'll look in the local databases. When was your victim killed?"

"In December of 1989."

Again, a clear and curious spark lit in her eyes. "Raped and stabbed, you said."

"Yes."

"How...um... How many times was she stabbed?"

Victor tilted his head and creased his brow, much as she had done while listening to him discuss the case. "Tell me why you care," he pressed. "And tell me the truth."

She looked like she was about to give him another line, but then she said, "There was a case at HEARTS. The woman was raped and murdered during a home invasion. Also in December 1989. She was stabbed multiple times. Brutally."

Victor held his breath as he processed that. He could see why she'd been so interested. Hope filled his chest. Maybe solving this case would be easier than he'd thought. He could practically hear the cha-ching of that reward money landing in the company account.

"Was anyone arrested?"

"No," she said in a way that made him think there was more to the story. "But the cases seem awfully similar, don't you think? And the timeline is awfully close together."

"I do think. I want to hear more about this case."

Sam shrugged. "I don't know much more than that. I had done a search of old police records looking for someone who fit the description."

He sensed she was holding out. For a moment he had a flash of fear that she would take what she knew of this case and give it to whomever was working the case at her old company. He didn't know her well enough to know that she wouldn't. He *hoped* she wouldn't, but he didn't *know*. If she went running to HEARTS, letting them know to look into Annette's case, that could give them the upper hand. Obviously, they'd been working this before him. Damn it.

"Give me more," he said.

"I don't—"

"Don't lie to me." Victor didn't mean for his voice to grow hard, but it had before he could stop it. "Don't ever lie to me, Sam. That is one thing I won't tolerate."

Her eyes filled with worry. She was torn. Obviously, she knew more, but she wasn't sure what to say. "The man who killed the victim had a tattoo on his right forearm. A black dagger. But they never found him."

"That's too bad," Victor said, hesitant to believe that was all Sam knew.

"Do you..." Sam took a breath. "Can I see the woman who was murdered?"

Victor paused before pushing himself from the door frame and walking to the table. He opened the file and waited for Sam to join him. Instead of focusing on her sweet scent, as he usually did when she was next to him, he tried to read her response. She almost looked relieved when she looked at the photo.

"What were you expecting?" he asked softly, hoping a kinder approach would pull more from her.

"What?" Sam asked after blinking and turning her focus to him.

He restrained the urge to snap at her. He wasn't kidding when he told her he wouldn't tolerate being lied to. "You were expecting something else?"

"No," she said unconvincingly. "Not exactly."

"What did the other victim look like?"

"Blond. I just..." She gestured at the photo of the young brunette who had been brutally murdered. "She was pretty."

He looked at the photo of the woman with dark hair and a bright smile. "Yes. She was."

"I'm sorry that her life ended that way." Her soft smile faded, and her eyes grew sad. "No one deserves to die like that. With so much pain and suffering." Her voice grew emotional at the end, as if she felt more than sympathy for this woman. Like she was hurting. It was more than pity. It sounded personal.

"No," he said suspiciously. "No one should die like that. I need you to tell me everything you can about the case HEARTS is working on."

She blinked at him. "Uh. That's all I know. Really."

"Sam."

"I was the receptionist, Victor. They didn't tell me much unless they needed me to look through records."

That felt like a lie. He wanted to call her out on it, but without another word, she slipped around him and out of the office. Victor stared at the woman's photo for several more seconds before focusing on the door where Sam had disappeared, convinced she still wasn't being completely honest with him.

[2]

Sam's heart started to pound as she pulled out of the E.I. parking lot. She didn't know why she felt the need to tell Holly what she suspected. She certainly didn't owe her old boss anything, least of all loyalty, but the chill that had settled over Sam's soul as she looked at the file on Annette Carlton was real. The evidence Victor had shared about the woman's brutal murder was real. And it was all too familiar.

The similarities between Annette's death and the horrific things Holly had witnessed so many years ago could not be ignored.

Holly had been looking for that man—the one who killed the woman in Victor's file—for a long time. And for incredibly personal reasons. Holly was just a little girl the night her mother had died. They'd been cuddled up on the sofa watching television when a man broke into their house. Her mother had told Holly to hide behind the couch.

Unfortunately, despite her hiding spot, Holly was able to see what had transpired. At just eight years old, she'd witnessed her mother get raped and repeatedly stabbed until she'd bled to death. The man hadn't known Holly was hiding or she likely would have died too. Though she had lived, the trauma was something Holly carried with her every day. There was always a shadow hanging over her.

Survivor's guilt had molded her into the person she was today—cool, aloof, but incredibly protective. That rough-around-the-edges persona was what Sam collided with most often. Holly had once told her if she'd ever lived through a real trauma, she'd grow up. Sam couldn't dispute that. Her life had been fairly smooth sailing considering what Holly had been through.

Despite the fight Sam and Holly had, Sam would never be able to stomach withholding that information from Holly. Especially now that Victor knew HEARTS had worked a similar case.

It was probably only a matter of time before he paid her former employer a visit to ask what they knew.

Holly never was comfortable talking about what happened to her mother, and Sam highly doubted she would appreciate it if Victor popped in to ask her about that night so long ago. So, Sam would explain as gently as possible what she'd learned and how much she'd shared—which wasn't a lot. Then, assuming she and Holly could have a civilized conversation about this, Sam would share her suspicions that Holly and Victor were looking for the same man. She would ask if Holly wanted to talk to Victor and maybe collaborate with E.I. so they could put their collective heads together and hopefully solve this case. Or maybe Holly would like to hand her information to him. Or whatever Holly wanted to do.

However, the closer Sam got to the HEARTS office, the less confident she felt. She and Holly hadn't ever been on great terms—Holly thought Sam didn't take her job seriously enough, and Sam thought Holly was way too serious. But the last time they'd seen each other had ended in a screaming match over the plans Sam had made for Holly's wedding.

Holly hadn't wanted a fancy wedding but had agreed to let Sam make it at least nice. When Sam had called the tailor and asked for the slit in Holly's dress to be extended a few inches to allow for the first dance, the tailor had called Holly to verify. And Holly had gone ballistic.

Everyone had taken Holly's side, insisting that Sam had overstepped her wedding planner duties. Maybe she had, but Holly had given her permission to make the wedding plans as painless as possible. In fact, Holly had said she didn't want to be consulted unless she absolutely had to be.

They hadn't spoken since that blowup. Almost two weeks ago. Sam couldn't recall a time when she and Holly had gone more than a day without speaking. The idea of seeing her now made Sam's palms sweat.

Relief filled Sam when she pulled into the familiar parking lot and realized Holly's car wasn't there. She parked in her old spot and hopped out of her car, taking her tablet with her to tap notes into. Even if Holly weren't there to give her more information, everyone at HEARTS was familiar with the case. Everyone wanted Holly to find the man who had murdered her mother so she could make peace with the past.

She was equally as relieved that the new receptionist wasn't there to greet her. Seeing someone else sit at her old desk would have felt like a slap she didn't need. Tika had told her that Susan, a witness in an old case, had been hired to fill her position. Sam didn't resent Susan for that. The woman had been through hell, and Sam was glad to see her taking back a little piece of her life, even if it was by sitting in Sam's old chair. But that didn't mean Sam actually wanted to see her sitting there.

Sam slipped down the hall and poked her head into Tika Brown's office. While Sam loved all of the HEARTS, Tika had been her work bestie for two years.

"Yo, bitch," Sam said lightly. "What's up?"

Tika looked up and grinned. "I hope you brought food. I haven't taken a break yet."

"I didn't even think about it."

"Want to go grab something?" Tika asked, already standing.

For the first time since deciding to head to HEARTS, Sam had a realization that maybe she didn't belong here any longer. Like she wasn't welcome. Why did Tika seem to be in such a hurry to get her out of there? Sam's smile faded and butterflies filled her stomach. "Actually, um..."

"Hey, stranger," Alexa said as she strode down the hallway.

Sam managed a smile. "Hey. How are you feeling?"

Alexa put a hand low on her stomach and blew out a breath. "Abuela insists the morning sickness will end soon, but I keep thinking of those poor women who vomit right up through birth. I don't think I'll survive if I'm one of those."

"I hear crackers help."

"I've tried every kind of cracker I can find. I've come to believe that's a myth." She tilted her head and her smile softened. "What are you doing here?"

Again, Sam's confidence wavered. This time in her decision to share information about Victor's case, but she couldn't keep this new knowledge to herself. Even if Holly were mad at her, even if she no longer fit in at HEARTS, Sam wouldn't withhold information that could lead to giving Holly the peace of mind she needed.

Lifting her tablet with the E.I. logo on the back, she tapped it as if it were evidence. "I got a new job. At Estrada Investigations."

"Boo!" Eva called from across the hall as she came to lean on the doorjamb of her office. "They're a bunch of used jockstraps."

Sam smirked. She couldn't deny that assessment. Javier and Conner rarely talked about anything but sports, but those jockstraps were her crew now.

"Victor Estrada works cold cases."

"Because he's the biggest jockstrap of all," Eva said. "I've had to deal with them." Eva had left her job at the police department because, as a beautiful petite female, she wasn't taken seriously. She more than made up for her stature with attitude. While she might be cute as a damn pixie, she certainly wasn't as sweet as one. She'd kick anyone's ass just to prove it.

"The case he's working now," Sam said hesitantly, "a woman was raped and stabbed to death during a home invasion." Tension filled the small space where Sam stood with her former teammates. "She was killed in December 1989. Less than a week after Holly's mom died."

"Holy shit," Eva breathed.

"Suspects?" Alexa asked.

"A neighbor saw a tall bald man walking down the street, but the police never found him. He wasn't ever considered a suspect."

"Tall and bald," Eva muttered.

She didn't have to say more. They all knew the man who Holly had seen kill her mother fit that description.

"Nothing else?" Alexa asked.

Sam shook her head. "That's it. I know it's not a lot, but it's still too much of a coincidence. Don't you think?"

"Definitely," Tika said. "Why wasn't this linked to Holly's mom? Why didn't the police make this connection?"

"Annette didn't live close to Holly. Probably different departments."

"But Holly's been scouring reports and records for years," Eva said softly. "How did she miss this?"

"She's too close to it," Alexa offered. "I know the reason I haven't found out what happened to Lanie is because I'm looking too hard at the wrong things. Holly and I have been helping each other out, trying to see things from new angles, but there's too much information for us to see everything."

Tika shook her head. "When the cases are this old, there's no way to tell how well the records were done and where they were kept. It's not like today when everything gets uploaded to a drive automatically. Back then, we had to rely on paper records. Things fell through cracks."

"Did you tell Victor?" Eva asked.

Sam sighed, knowing she was walking a fine line of betrayal with her new boss. "I told him I'd seen a similar case at HEARTS, but I didn't tell him it was Holly's mom. I...I thought it should be Holly's decision if she wanted to talk to him."

"You can't tell Holly," Alexa stated quickly. "Not right now. She's super stressed out with the wedding and..." She glanced at Sam. "Sorry, babe. But...you know. She's stressed. This will send her spiraling, and none of us needs that, least of all Holly."

"So..." Sam drawled as she looked at her friends. "What do I do?"

Eva smirked, as if the answer was obvious. "Solve the case. Save the day. Make Holly forgive you so you can come home."

"I like my new job," Sam said defiantly. However, she suspected that every single one of them knew as well as she did that if Holly offered to let her come back, she'd probably jump at the chance. "But I will see if I can help solve the case. Because Holly deserves to know the truth. *Not* because I need her forgiveness."

Alexa moaned. "God, you two are like children." She walked away, muttering under her breath in Spanish. She always switched to Spanish when she didn't want her teammates to understand her, but Sam had enough familiarity with the language to pick up a few cuss words.

A moment later, Alexa appeared with a manila folder. "I'll get you a copy of this."

"I'm on it," Tika said, taking the folder from her.

As soon as Tika rushed off, Alexa said, "That folder has

all my notes. Do not and I mean *do not* share them with Victor Estrada. Those are Holly's personal recollections of the night she saw her mom die in the most horrific way imaginable. It's personal and traumatizing, but I'm trusting you with it because if you can add even one more piece of the puzzle, it will be worth it."

"I agree," Sam said.

"Don't tell him anything about Holly," Eva warned. "He's an egotistical prick, and she would be pissed if you talked to him about her."

"He's not that bad," Sam said, feeling the need to defend her new boss.

"Whatever," Eva said. "And keep him away from Holly unless she gives the green light to talk to him. If he barges in here to question her, she really will never forgive you."

Sam frowned when Eva lifted a ginger brow to emphasize the warning. "I know she wouldn't. I'll redact her name just in case he finds my notes."

"Good plan." Alexa put her hand on Sam's shoulder and stared at her with soothing brown eyes. "We've been worried about you. Are you okay?"

"I'm fine," she said but was certain they saw through her. While she had landed a great job and loved knowing she would eventually have a bigger role on her new team, she missed her friends. There was so much laughter at the HEARTS office. Eva kept a bottle of vodka in the freezer and offered up shots whenever anyone was having a bad day. Tika was always good for cake. And Rene, though so much like Holly, was good for advice.

Sam definitely hadn't settled into that kind of rapport

with her new team. She hoped she would someday, but until she learned to like sports, she would never fit in at E.I. She missed these women. She missed this place.

"Here you go," Tika said and handed a file to Sam before giving the original to Alexa.

"Keep us posted," Alexa said. "Or if you need help…"

"I know," Sam said with a soft smile. "I'm going to go before…" She swallowed hard. She wanted to ask about wedding plans and the baby Alexa only recently learned she was carrying. Instead, she turned and left her old team to muse about whatever they would muse about in her absence.

Even so, once Sam got into her car and slid her dark sunglasses on, a smile curved her lips. She glanced at the file on the seat next to her.

She had a case—*unofficially*—and she wasn't going to stop until she'd solved it.

Victor didn't bother looking up to see who was standing in his office doorway. He and his brother shared a connection that didn't need verification.

"What is it, Javier?"

"What's going on with you and the new girl?"

"Don't let Samantha hear you call her a girl. I doubt she'd appreciate that."

"We agreed we needed a woman on the team to diversify and reach more clients. Not so you had easy prey."

Victor let out a low whistle as he sat back and finally eyed his little brother. "*Prey?*"

"You know what I mean."

"Did you want her?"

Javier sighed and frowned. When he did that, he reminded Victor of their mother. Mama had always been so exacerbated with Victor. Even as a child, he tended to be drawn to trouble like a compass needle to true north. The resemblance between Javier and Mama made him smile. Though she'd been gone for several years, she would be proud of her youngest for the dramatic reaction he'd had to Victor's latest behavior.

"Shall we flip a coin?" Victor asked, just to poke at Javier.

"It's not a game," Javier stated, "and she's not a prize."

"I didn't say she was."

"Yet you've been sniffing around her since the day she started like she's a prized hen."

Tired of the conversation, Victor tossed his pen down. "What's wrong with you?"

"She's smart. Valuable. And she's the first female we've ever had on the team."

"What about Lorraine?"

Javier didn't budge. "Don't run her off."

No longer amused, Victor said, "I have no intention of running her off."

"Then stop flirting with her."

Victor frowned. He liked Sam. More than he should. There was a pull between them that he wasn't foolish enough to call more than something physical. Lust was lust. With Sam, though, it was strong. Primal almost.

When he looked at her, he wanted to know that no other man would be looking at her. That was ridiculous. He wasn't the kind of man who wanted to possess a woman. Hell, if anything, he was the love 'em and leave 'em type.

However, there was something about Sam. Maybe the sadness just beneath the surface. Maybe the determination that always seemed to find her at the last moment. Maybe the fact that she was easily one of the most beautiful women he'd ever seen, and she was right there within reach. He hoped it wasn't simply the last reason. He hoped he was better than that, but honestly, he couldn't think straight enough to know for certain. She had him wound up in ways he couldn't explain.

The connection he felt to Sam was odd, and he didn't like it, but he couldn't deny it.

"I mean it," Javier stated. "Stop before it goes too far and we lose her."

"I second that," Conner said walking into the room. He slipped by Javier and dropped into a chair in front of Victor's desk. "It took her all of five minutes to search and find the records I had been needing. She's good at her job. Damn good. We need her here. Besides, she's too good for you."

"Why are you two busting my balls right now?" Victor asked as he sank back in the chair.

"We saw the way you were looking at her as she left," Conner said.

Victor chuckled. "And how was that?"

"Like you wanted to follow her," Javier stated.

"Oh, I did want to follow her," Victor said. "But not for the reason that you two apparently think. Did either of you happen to notice how she perked up when I started talking about this new cold case I'm looking into?" He looked between his coworkers. "No? Maybe that's why I'm always picking up your slack on your research."

"Screw you, dude," Conner muttered. "We noticed. Why do you think we hustled out of there?"

"To give you time to get to the bottom of it. Did you?" Javier asked, ignoring his older brother's jab.

"She knows something about that case. When I cornered her before she left, she admitted it sounded familiar to a case one of the investigators at HEARTS had been looking into, but she danced around telling me anything. Then she practically ran out of here. So yeah, I did want to follow her. But not for any other reason than to know exactly where she went after she left here."

"Why didn't you?" Conner asked.

"Because, according to you two—the assholes who came in here to warn me off my employee—I don't trust people enough."

"You don't," Javier and Conner said in unison.

"So I'm giving our new teammate the benefit of the doubt. Let her get her thoughts together, because she was obviously shaken, and then I'll wait. And she had better," he stated firmly, "come straight to me and tell me what she knows or we're going to have a talk about loyalty."

"He's going to run her off," Javier muttered as he turned to leave.

"Yup." Conner stood and followed suit.

Victor shook his head. If left up to them, they'd let everyone get away with everything. Turning his attention back to the file on his desk, he lost himself in trying to piece together exactly what had happened to Annette

Carlton from the very few witness statements in the police report.

Given the amount of violence Annette faced in the last minutes of her life, it certainly didn't seem like the police had been overly concerned about finding the man responsible. That made Victor wonder if there was more to her past than met the eye.

He was searching old police reports, wondering if she had an arrest record, when Sam knocked on his office door.

Victor smiled, happy that she was, he assumed, there to explain her reaction earlier.

"May I come in?" she asked.

He gestured to the chair across from him. He did his best to hold her gaze as she sat. Even if Javier and Conner hadn't called him out, he had chastised himself for his blatant flirting with Sam. She hadn't worked with him long enough to be acting like a lovesick Casanova. And Javier was right, she deserved to be treated like part of the team. So...hard as it was going to be, Victor was going to do his best to treat her like that.

"I went to HEARTS to talk to the investigator who had been looking into the case similar to yours."

Victor practically wanted to jump up and high-five her... or hug her...or more...because she'd passed the test he'd set out before.

Instead, he nodded sagely. "And?"

"She isn't willing to share. Yet," she added quickly when he scoffed. "But I have access to information on her case, so I can—"

"No," Victor stated.

Sam leaned back. "What do you mean *no*? You didn't even let me finish."

"You were going to say you can share my case with them."

"No, I wasn't." She put her hand to her chest as if offended. "I would never share your case—"

"So what did you tell this former coworker of yours when you asked about her case?"

Sam was quiet for a moment. "I told her you had a similar case. But I didn't give her any details."

"And she just gave you access to her case?"

Frustration lit on her face. "There are two women who were terrorized in the last moments of their lives, Victor. And there is a very real possibility that the man responsible is still out there somewhere. Even if he isn't, if we can bring closure to these two families, we have to do whatever it takes to do that. I'm not going to share your information any more than I'm going to share the information from HEARTS, but if I can be the intermediary and pull everything together—"

"Then you go solve the case."

"Wow," she said softly. "They were right about you. You are an egomaniac."

He blinked, not sure how to respond to that. This certainly wasn't the first time he'd been told that, not even the first time he'd been told that to his face, but he hadn't expected it from Sam. And at this moment, when he was uncertain of her motives.

She seemed far too eager to solve this case, and he had to wonder why. And, as much as he didn't want to think it, he had to question her loyalty to his company. Maybe she had seen this as an opportunity to get her old job back. She hadn't been shy about telling him that she'd left after a personal conflict with Holly Austin.

Victor didn't know Holly well, but he could see how that was possible. The woman was about as warm as a frozen fish stick. But conflicts could be resolved. Friendships could mend. And he didn't want to see this case, or the reward, walk out of his office and right back to HEARTS because he was too trusting of this new addition to his staff.

"It's not about my ego," Victor finally said.

"Then what is it about?"

He drew a breath as he debated sharing his concerns. "There's a nice reward tied to this case."

"Which will still be paid to E.I."

"What about HEARTS? Don't they want a cut?"

Sam seemed to consider that for a moment before shaking her head. "No. They want peace for the family of the victims."

"How noble," he said flatly.

"Are you seriously willing to miss out on breaking this case wide open because you think someone else might get credit?"

That felt like a kick to the gut and a test of his ethics. Was he? Would he really let a rapist and murderer go free because of his pride? Picking up the file on Annette Carlton's case, he eyed Sam.

"Ask Lorraine to make a copy of this for you. But if you share so much as a photo from this file with anyone outside of this agency, you will be escorted out of E.I., and you will never be welcomed back. Do you understand?"

"Completely." Standing, she snatched the file from him and started for the door. Before leaving, she turned and stared him down. "We need to find him, Victor," she stated. "This is the most logical way."

He didn't agree or disagree. He simply sat there, wondering what it was that she still wasn't telling him.

[3]

Sam's eyes burned from staring at the computer screen for so long. She'd looked at so many photos from the public digital records of old arrests that she could barely make out the faces any longer. The more she tried to find the man who killed the woman in Victor's file—and possibly Holly's mother—the less she could recall what he looked like. She had to continually look at her notes because every face made her question what she was looking for.

After a while, a thug was a thug was a thug. They all started to blend together, and she was questioning information that she knew like the back of her hand. Rene, one of the HEARTS, had told Sam a hundred times not to second-guess herself. Rene told her to keep her head up and go confidently about her business.

Rubbing her eyes, Sam couldn't help but wonder if Rene had had this information, if she would have found the killer by now.

Looking at the clock in the corner of her laptop, she blew

out a long breath. She'd been at this for hours. No wonder she couldn't think—or see—straight any longer. After tilting her head from side to side, she rolled her shoulders to try to ease the tension in her neck.

She'd gone back as far as the late 1970s and stared at hundreds of men who fit the description, weeding through identifiers, desperate to find someone with a dagger tattoo like the one Holly had seen the night her mom had been murdered.

She was in the mid-1990s before realizing that Holly would have done this. She would have obsessed over this. Her fiancé, Jack, probably would have done this too. As a detective at a local police station, he would have had access to all these files. If there was something there to be found, someone would have found it by now.

So what made Sam think she'd actually find the guy?

Falling back in her chair, she blew out a long breath as her confidence faded. Frustrated, she logged into the company database and opened the file Victor had on Annette's murder. Rather than focusing on the night she was murdered, she read through the police report and witness statements. What few witnesses there were that had anything to offer.

She read the file twice before tossing it aside. Everything pointed to this being random. No one seemed to have anything against Annette. She was sweet. Quiet. Unobtrusive.

No one seemed to have any reason to hurt her.

Sam was about ready to rip her hair out. This couldn't be another dead end. Another false lead. She felt in her heart that this was somehow connected to what Holly had witnessed so many years ago. The women's deaths were far too similar to be a coincidence.

"What are you missing?" Sam whispered.

Rather than continue to beat her head against the wall, she gave in and dialed her phone.

"Hey, chick," Eva answered. "What's up?"

"If you were trying to solve a cold case, what would be your first step?"

"After reading the file?"

Sam laughed softly. "Okay. What would be your second step?"

"Track down any living witnesses and question them again. They could have withheld information, intentionally or not, during the initial questioning. After time, shock wears off, worries abate, guilt takes a toll. If someone wasn't being honest the first time around, they might be willing to share what they know now."

After clicking her tongue, Sam said, "You're brilliant and I love you."

"Love you," Eva said as Sam ended the call.

Opening the file again, she started tracking down the witnesses in the file. Several were dead, one had moved to another state, but according to a search of local property records, two of Annette's neighbors still lived in the same houses. Sam would start there. Hopefully, at least one of them would be willing to tell her something.

"I'm heading out to follow some leads," she said to Lorraine and slid a piece of paper across the desk.

Lorraine peered at it. "What's this?"

"The addresses where I'll be."

"Why do I need that?"

Sam looked at her curiously. HEARTS had an unbreakable rule about making sure someone knew where the investigators were headed.

"In case I disappear without a trace. You know where to start looking."

Lorraine took the paper. "Oh. Good plan. Thanks."

Rather than explaining further, Sam left. She considered how flippant E.I. was about the safety of their staff. Of course, Sam was the first female investigator, so maybe they had some macho man belief that nothing bad could ever happen to them. She'd have to talk to Victor about implementing some safety measures. But she'd wait until she'd been there longer. She hadn't even made it a month. It seemed a bit premature to start pointing out the shortcomings of his business.

Half an hour later, Sam was pulling up in front of the house where Annette had died. She took a moment of silence to send up a silent promise to the woman to do her best to find her killer.

If you have any pointers, Sam added to her vow, *feel free to throw them my way.*

Annette's former neighbor answered Sam's second knock. The older woman looked suspiciously through the window, so Sam put on her sweetest smile.

"Mrs. Mayer?"

"Yeah," the woman said around her frown.

"I'm so sorry to bother you. My name is Samantha Turner. I'm a private investigator. I'm working on an old case. May I ask you a few questions about Annette Carlton?"

The woman's breath caught, and she swayed slightly on her feet. "My God. I haven't heard that name in years."

"I apologize for springing this on you," Sam said.

Mrs. Mayer looked around, as if to make sure no one was watching, before ushering Sam inside. The house looked like it hadn't been updated much since the '90s, the time when Annette had been killed. Mauve and hunter green dominated the color scheme, making it look outdated but nostalgic.

Sam sat on the flower-patterned sofa while Mrs. Mayer sat in a worn recliner. That was clearly her seat of choice.

"I was sitting right here when I noticed him," Mrs. Mayer said softly. She stared out the big window of her living room as if being transported back in time. "I watched him for a few minutes, wondering why he was standing outside smoking, but then the commercial break ended, and I looked at the television. When I looked out the window again, he was gone, and I didn't give him another thought until the police showed up two days later after Annette's boss called and asked them to do a wellness check." She shook her head and blinked at Sam. Her cloudy gray eyes were filled with sadness. "I told them all about him, but they didn't seem convinced he had anything to do with what happened to that girl."

"This was the tall bald man?"

Mrs. Mayer nodded. "I didn't get a very good look at him, you understand? He was looking across the street at Annette's house. He looked down the street once when I was watching him, but... I didn't get a very good look at him. A tall bald man smoking a cigarette. That's all I had to offer them. It wasn't much."

Sam didn't disagree. "Can you tell me more about Annette? Do you know why anyone would want to hurt her?"

"Oh, no," Mrs. Mayer said gently. "She was the sweetest young thing. She'd come from a really rough background. Her father was into drugs and gambling. He had come around a time or two trying to get money from her, but she wouldn't give him a dime. Not a dime," she stated firmly. "He'd get mad as hell and stand outside screaming. Annette would always bring over cookies after one of his visits and apologize for the fuss. She did that for all the neighbors. We all felt sorry for her and started keeping an eye out for him. Someone would call the cops if we saw him hanging around. For her sake."

Sam nodded. "Of course."

"I think that's why it was so tragic for us all when she died. We thought we were looking out for her."

"It sounds like you tried."

Mrs. Mayer sighed. "I wish I could tell you more. She deserves to have her murderer put behind bars, but unfortunately, I don't know anyone who would intentionally hurt her. Her father was questioned, but they never arrested him, so he must not have had anything to do with it."

The woman didn't sound convinced, but Sam didn't want to push. She'd look into Annette's father on her own.

"Is there anything else you can think of that might help me?"

The woman shook her head. "Honey, if I had any idea, I would have told the police a long time ago. I wish I could help."

"You've done plenty," Sam said with a smile. She pulled a card from her pocket and put it on the coffee table. "If you do think of anything, please don't hesitate to call me. Thank you for your time."

"Thank you," Mrs. Mayer said. "And good luck."

Sam went to the house next door to Mrs. Mayer and spoke with the man who lived there. He hadn't been home when Annette had died. His wife had spoken to the police, but she'd since passed, and he wasn't keen on discussing the matter. He barely even opened the door. Rather than press him, Sam smiled, thanked him for his time, and climbed into her car.

She'd passed a small coffee shop on her way into the neighborhood, so she went back there and carried her bag inside. With a small mocha at her side, she dug into her notes and started researching Annette Carlton's father.

It was closing in on seven o'clock when Sam barged into Victor's office. He jumped, nearly yelped, because he had thought he was the only one still in the office. Lorraine left at five o'clock sharp, and the other two jackasses were usually not far behind her. Victor was used to having the office to himself this late in the evening.

Putting his hand to his chest, he blew out a breath as he eyed the woman before him.

The excitement on her face was undeniable and made him smile.

"Well, come on in," he said sarcastically because she was already marching across to his desk.

"In 2001, the police busted a loan shark ring. These were the lowest of the low. The bottom of the barrel. The scummiest of the scummy."

"Okay," he drawled.

"These guys would ensnare people with money problems, anyone from gambling debt to overdue mortgages." She dropped into the chair across from him. "Then, they'd charge a crazy amount of interest, making sure these people could never pay the debt."

"As loan sharks do," he said, not understanding why he should care about this.

"And then they'd sell that debt to organized crime organizations. It was like a victim assembly line for the freaking mafia. Loop in the little guy who couldn't pay his bills, get him in over his head, and then sell him to the next guy up the line."

Victor nodded slightly. "Okay?" he asked again.

"Know whose name came up when the police started digging through the victims?"

"Annette Carlton?" he asked hesitantly. Mafia debt didn't seem to fit the profile of what he knew about Annette.

Sam shook her head. "Roger Carlton. Annette's father."

Victor creased his brow. "What does that have to do with Annette?"

"Do you know what happens when you owe organized crime and you don't pay up?"

"They beat you up?"

"They beat up the people you care about. Like your daughter."

Victor sat taller. "And maybe sometimes that beating gets out of control."

"And maybe your daughter dies because of your fuck-ups." Her face grew sober. "According to the police files, Roger Carlton's debt was erased less than a week after his daughter was murdered."

"Son of a bitch," Victor muttered. "Where is Roger Carlton?"

Sam shrugged. "I haven't tracked him down yet. But I think this is worth looking into, don't you? I think we need to question him about this debt."

Victor nodded. "Whoa. Wait a second. How did you get this much information about a police case?"

Sam's smile returned. "Don't ask me questions like that, Victor."

"I think I need to know."

"No. You don't." She pushed herself up. "I'm going to track daddy dearest down. I want to know what he knows about his daughter's death."

"Don't talk to him without me," Victor said, getting up. He walked around the desk and stared her down. "I don't want you confronting someone who might panic. Nothing happens to you on my watch, okay."

She tilted her head and smirked. "About that..."

"Yeah, Lorraine gave me your note and asked why we weren't doing this sooner. She's already planning to implement babysitting steps for us."

"It's not babysitting," Sam stated. "It's a safety precaution."

"We should...discuss this in more depth. And I think I owe you dinner for this new information you've found. A thank you, if you will."

He didn't mean for heat to fill his eyes, but even he realized he was all but trying to seduce her. And in a way that he'd laugh at if he'd see his brother or Conner trying it. But Sam didn't laugh or point out he was crossing a line. In fact, she didn't say anything.

Victor should have known better, but he did it anyway. Sam watched, looking absolutely luscious, as Victor leaned his face toward hers. He hesitated, searching her eyes for permission, before putting his lips on hers. She didn't confirm she wanted this to happen, but she didn't stop him either, so he pulled her closer.

When he finally put his lips on hers, he felt like he was coming home. He was so nervous, it reminded him of the first time he'd ever kissed someone he had a crush on. Usually, he was so confident, so sure of himself, but something about this woman made him question everything.

Victor dug his hands into her hair, holding her as he parted his lips and deepened the kiss. Sliding his hand around her waist, he pulled her against him as she tightened her arms around his neck. Feeling her passion ignite made him pull her even closer, and he couldn't help the way he ground his body into hers. The sudden awareness of what he'd been missing seemed to take over his senses.

Pulling back, he held her head between his hands, searching her eyes while they both took a moment to gasp for oxygen. Her eyes were a dark-blue shade that was an instant betrayal to any attempt she might have of hiding her desires. She wanted him like he wanted her.

He didn't speak as he released her. There was a silent agreement between them.

"It's just about closing time," he whispered. "We can't work all the time. We have to take a break at some point."

Sam grinned. "A break?"

"Yeah," he practically growled. "Would you like to meet me at my place?"

She grinned. "Yeah. I think I would."

He hesitated, ignoring the warnings his coworkers had issued, and grabbed a sticky note off his desk. After jotting down his address, he handed it to her.

"I'll see you there in half an hour or so?"

Sam grinned. "I'll see you." She turned and glided out of his office.

Victor licked his lips as he watched her leave. This was a terrible idea, but he didn't care. There was something between them, and now that he knew she felt it as well, he didn't want to wait. He wouldn't risk letting her slip through his fingers. He didn't know why he had that feeling, but he did, and it was strong.

Something in the back of his mind told him his time with her was going to be brief and he needed to soak up all of her that he could. Grabbing his laptop and case files—because he always worked in the evenings—he rushed out of the office before anyone could pick up on his excitement and figure out what was about to transpire.

Doubt didn't start creeping into his own mind until he

got home and decided to order delivery. Only then did he realize he had no idea what he should order for his soon-to-be guest and lover. He had no idea what she would eat. Closing his eyes, he tried to recall what she'd eaten the day he'd taken her to lunch to welcome her to the company. All he could remember was how she licked her lips after every bite.

Damn.

Okay. No big deal. He'll ask her when she gets there. Offer to feed her before...other things.

However, when she arrived, and he opened the door to find her standing there, being a gentleman and buying her dinner first went out the window.

She'd touched up her make-up. More than touched it up. It was different. More dramatic. Sexier.

Damn and damn again. She certainly knew how to play him. And he liked that.

Taking her hand, he pulled her into his house and straight into his arms. Dinner could wait. "I want to be clear in saying that you don't have to do this. If you don't want..."

She put her fingers to his lips. "I'm here because I want to be here."

"Okay," he said and turned to move deeper into his house. Silently, she followed him up the stairs. In his room, he kicked the door closed behind him as he walked into the bedroom. The only light was coming from the full moon outside, but it was enough that when he laid her on the bed, he could see the lusty daze in her eyes.

She watched in the blue hue of the moonlight as he stared down at her while unbuttoning his shirt. After tossing it aside, he started on her shirt, moving painfully slow as he released the buttons, then pushed the soft material aside. He took a moment to look at her pale skin, her breasts covered by satin, before letting his fingers drift over her neck and stomach.

Every muscle in her body clenched, causing her to jump slightly. He liked the reaction. He looked into her eyes and smiled slightly, then used his fingers to release the clasp on her slacks and deftly slid the zipper down. Again, he parted the material and let his fingers touch the freshly exposed area before sliding his hand down her thigh and clutching the material of her pants in his hand. He watched her breasts heaving with her quick breaths for a moment before slowly leaning down to put his nose to her neck.

That warm, rosy scent that seemed to define her filled his senses. Kissing the spot just below her ear, he whispered his desire for her and felt her slipping deeper into the seductive web he was weaving. Her arms wrapped around him, and her legs intertwined with his when he slowly started moving his kisses downward. A moan escaped her, sending ripples through his body, as he pressed his lips just below her belly button. Clutching her hips, he lifted them slightly so he could slide her pants down. After dropping her slacks and shoes on the floor, Victor knelt beside the bed.

Grabbing her hands, he gently sat her up and cupped her face in his palms. Their eyes said everything it seemed they couldn't vocalize anymore, and both smiled slightly before he leaned in and kissed her again.

While Victor reached behind her to release her bra, Sam unbuckled his belt and undid the button and zipper. Gravity did its part by pulling his pants to the floor as he tossed aside the flimsy material that had covered her from his view.

A sound close to a growl escaped Sam as he grasped her breast and took her nipple between his lips, flicking it gently with his tongue. He suckled one side and then the other before nudging her back so his kisses fell over her stomach and then the band of her panties.

The mews escaping her as she fought to keep her control were almost enough to make him crazy, but he was determined that this was going to be the best damn make-up sex they'd ever had. In order to do that, he had to keep the pace slow and deliberate.

"My God, get on with it," Sam whispered.

He smiled and instead exhaled hot breath against her and brushed his nose over her pubic bone. She grasped the blankets in her fists and thrust her hips.

Gripping her thighs, Victor pressed his fingers into her to ease her down. Then he ran his hands down her legs, taking her underwear with them. Again, he closed his eyes and inhaled. He could smell her excitement and feel the warmth radiating from her. Brushing his nose and lips against the inside of her leg, he knew she must be cursing him for his torture. He knew exactly what she wanted and how she wanted it, but he wasn't going to give it to her until he was ready.

Turning his head to kiss the other leg, he again exhaled, causing her hips to lift once more. Looking up at her body, he saw her hands roaming over her breasts before she bit the knuckle of one finger.

Oh, yes, it was going to be a good night.

Kissing his way up her thigh, he decided enough was enough. He was torturing himself just as much as he was Sam. It was time to get to the good stuff.

As her moans increased and grew louder, Victor knew she was nearing the edge and slid his fingers into her opening to push her over the cliff. Her legs tightened around him, and she arched her back off the bed. She released the death grip on his hair in exchange for wrapping her fingers around a heap of blanket.

She had just started to relax when he slithered up her body, kicking his pants off the rest of the way as he went. His socks somehow found their way to the floor along with her stockings as he covered her body with his. Reaching for his nightstand, he opened the drawer and pulled out a condom.

He looked down, seeing the plea in her eyes as he hovered over her writhing body while sliding the protection over his erection. Finally, he was ready. Leaning down he kissed her deeply, and she tilted her hips enough that he felt her ready for him. Moving his hips slowly forward, she welcomed him inside her. Both moaned from the sensation.

Victor tried desperately to retain the slow pace he had set for himself, but feeling her pulling him to her and her body tightening around him as he entered her over and over was more than he could bear. Add the smell of her sweat mixing with his and the sounds that filled his ears every time she panted, and he was a goner. Lost inside her and the sheets that were tangled around their legs, Victor gave in and let his body take over.

Nipping at her flesh and grasping whatever he happened to get a hold of, Victor quickened the pace of their love-making until it was a heated frenzy. When he felt the inevitable climax, their eyes locked, and their bodies fell into a natural rhythm until Victor collapsed on top of her breathless body.

After taking a moment to catch his breath, he looked at her to find her looking at him. Both chuckled breathlessly as they met for a quick kiss. Rolling onto her side, Sam curled into Victor's chest and closed her eyes as he wrapped his arm around her. He couldn't recall ever holding a woman and not wanting to let her go, but in that moment, he would have done anything to keep Sam with him.

And that terrified him.

[4]

As soon as she'd woken up in Victor's bed, Sam had an overwhelming sense of guilt and shame and self-loathing wash over her. She'd never been good at self-control, but this was bad. This was so bad. The sex had been good. The sex had been worth it. But the situation...waking up naked in her boss's bed? After a week of him being her boss? That was bad. Worse than bad, it was stupid. She'd committed yet another one of her so-called blow jobs.

She slipped silently from his side, grabbed the articles of her clothing that were scattered about, and tiptoed to his living room where she dressed and sneaked from his house as quietly as possible.

Sam was no stranger to waking up with men she had no intention of starting a relationship with, but normally she didn't run from mornings like this. Normally, she'd laugh it off. Normally, she knew the guy was on the same page.

She was certain Victor had no expectations of a long-term romance, but that meant this had been a one-night stand. Between her and her boss. And that left her feeling unusually awkward.

Sam rushed through the shower once she got home and put on leggings and an oversized sweatshirt. Then she texted Tika that she was on her way to their appointment. She wouldn't have time to stop for coffee, which was going to make her a bit grumbly, but that was the consequence of sleeping in...with her boss.

Sam muttered a curse under her breath as she grabbed her purse and rushed out to meet her friend at the spa where they had a standing appointment on the last Saturday of every month.

Within half an hour, Sam was lying face down on a padded table while a surprisingly strong petite woman worked the knots out of her muscles.

"This is so nice," Sam moaned as the masseuse pressed on her legs.

"Yeah," Tika sighed from her table. "It would be better if you told me what is on your mind."

"What do you mean?"

"You're full of dramatic sighs this morning. Why?"

Sam debated how much she wanted to tell the woman next to her. Some things shouldn't be shared...even between best friends. "Because life is too short, and we need to take a break from time to time and enjoy it."

Tika sighed as she lifted her head. "Did you come up with that all on your own?"

Sam flashed to a memory of Victor telling her they needed to take a break from work before inviting her to his house. And they both knew why. A shaky breath left her as she recalled what that so-called break had led to.

"Actually, no."

"No?"

"This case is...depressing."

Pushing herself up slightly, Tika grunted when her masseuse pushed her back down. "All of our cases are depressing. Why is this one getting to you?"

"I guess...because it's possibly tied to Holly's mom. We've all tiptoed around this information for so long, and now...now I'm eyeballs deep in it, and it's...sad. I'm sad. For Holly and for this other woman."

Tika was quiet for a moment. "It's hard on Holly, but she's okay. She's handled it as well as anybody could."

"I know."

"Did you learn something new? Is that what this is about?"

As much as Sam wanted to toss what she'd learned about Annette's dad out there to see if Tika thought there could have been similar issues with Holly's parents, she didn't dare. Victor had made it clear there were boundaries, and Sam was determined to respect them.

Though he didn't seem to have boundaries anywhere else. Not that she could talk. She had been just as flirty and had gone to his house knowing exactly what she was doing and what was going to happen.

"Maybe it isn't about the case as much as..."

"What?" Tika pressed with a grunt. Her masseuse was definitely not as gentle as Sam's, which made Sam chuckle.

"I might be a little in over my head."

"It's way too soon to think that," Tika said. "You just got all the information. I felt the same way when I was working my first case. I felt completely incompetent. I know you aren't officially part of the team anymore," she said gently, "but we're here for you. All of us. All you have to do is ask."

"Um...yeah, I know. I appreciate that, but... I didn't mean I was in over my head with the case as much as...maybe with...Victor."

Tika gasped and popped herself up on her elbows, ignoring the woman behind her trying to get her to lie back down. "Why would you be in over your head with Victor?" Tika asked, her eyes wide as if she knew. Hell, they were best friends. She totally knew.

Sam sighed. "Never mind."

"Uh, no. Not never mind. Dish," Tika insisted.

Sam laughed slightly. "There is no dish."

"You are a terrible liar." Easing down, she pressed her face into the space available and silently waited. She always silently waited until Sam couldn't wait to spill the beans. But Sam did wait. At least until their massages had ended and they were in the locker room getting dressed.

As she pulled her pants up, Sam said, "I slept with him."

Tika stopped dressing as she turned to face her friend. "Him? Be specific."

"Who do you think?"

Tugging her shirt down, Tika crossed her arms, which didn't have the serious impact it would have if she'd put her pants on first. "You screwed your boss?"

"Yeah."

"After like a week?"

"Yup."

"Damn, girl. How are things between you now?"

Sam shrugged and slipped into her T-shirt. "Fine as far as I know."

"What led to this? So quickly?"

She finished dressing before sitting on a bench to put her shoes on. "I don't know. There's a spark there. I felt it when I first met him. I think…"

"What?" Tika pressed.

Chuckling, she shook her head. "I think he was forbidden fruit. I told myself from the first time I saw him that I wasn't going to give in, so…what do I do?"

"Went and got yourself a little taste of heaven," Tika teased.

Sam didn't want to laugh, but she couldn't stop the soft chuckle from leaving her. "He's been flirting with me since I started. Okay…we've been flirting with each other," she admitted. "A lot. I don't think either of us meant to give in, though. I was talking to him about the case last night, and he kissed me, invited me to his place, and that was it. Done. I slipped out this morning before he woke up."

"Just like that," Tika commented hesitantly. "Are you concerned where you stand with him now?"

Rolling her head toward Tika, Sam took a deep breath. "I don't think he's going to fire me, if that's what you mean."

"If he did, you could sue him for sexual harassment. I mean, without a doubt. Not that there's a limit on how much time has to pass between the sexual advance and the time of firing, but to do so in such a short time would pretty much seal the deal. Meaning, his ass would definitely be grass."

"Well, it's good to know I could nail him...figuratively this time...but I don't think he will." She finished tying her shoe and stood before she gave in and told Tika about the potential break in the case. Unless she needed input from HEARTS, she was going to keep a lid on this. She didn't want to give Victor a reason to get pissed at her.

Looking at her friend, Tika was obviously trying to tread lightly. "How long are you going to wait before you apologize to Holly and come back to HEARTS?"

Sam creased her brow as she turned her head sharply. "Look, I know I overstepped, but Holly did too. Why should I be the one to apologize?"

Tika sighed and rolled her eyes. "Because you're the bigger person."

"No, I'm not. And you don't even try to act like you believe that. Other than a nasty attitude, Holly's a freakin' saint."

A quiet giggle left Tika. "Hardly. She has her fair share of flaws."

"Not as many as me."

"Most people want to be the bigger person, Sam."

"Well, I don't. Not this time."

Wrapping her arm around Sam's shoulders, Tika outright laughed. "I swear, you two are more like sisters than any biological sisters I know."

Sam pouted. A few months ago, she would have felt honored to be Holly's sister. Now it wasn't the compliment it should have been.

"Holly is the least of my problems right now," Sam said. "I slept with my boss last night, Tika. What do I do now?"

"Was it good?"

"Incredible."

"Then don't do anything. Let things be and see where they go."

"No, no, no," Sam insisted as she jumped back up and grabbed what was left of her belongings from the locker. "I can't do that. I need to put an end to this before I get into any more trouble than I already am."

"Do you like him?"

Biting her lip, Sam took a deep breath before nodding. "I do. It's more than that, though. It's odd. I feel something very, very strong. Like I've never felt before."

"Sam, that is great!"

Sam wished she felt the same. Whatever was going on between her and Victor was unexpected and happening way too fast. "Yeah, except for the fact that I can't do anything about it because he's my boss."

Tika's eyes bulged. "Honey, I hate to break this to you, but you already did do something about it."

"I mean...I can't keep doing that. Continuing to sleep with him would just send a lot of mixed signals. Even if I had feelings for him, which I'm not saying I do, I'm just saying there's something..." Sam sighed when she realized she was rambling. "I can't keep sleeping with him, Tik. That's a bad idea no matter how I spin it."

"You think he's got feelings?"

"Neither of us have feelings, Tik," she said, backtracking because she refused to admit there were actual feelings involved so soon. "We have...lust. And that's not good. Not a week into my employment. He's going to fire me."

Putting her purse strap over her shoulder, Tika eyed her friend. "Why do you think that?"

"Because neither of us are long-term relationship material, and he isn't going to quit his company when this ends. One of us will have to go. It'll be me."

"So what are you going to do?" Tika asked.

"I have to end things. I have to tell him last night was great, but it can't happen again."

"And if he fires you?"

Sam shrugged. "He won't."

"How can you be so sure?"

"Because I have information on the case he's working on that he needs."

Tika simply stared at her. "For now."

"Well, now is all I need. By the time we solve this case, I'll have proved I'm worth more than sex. He'll keep me. I have to tell him that last night was a one-time thing. It can't happen again."

"But you want it to happen again. Don't you?"

"God, yes," Sam sighed. She stood taller, lifting her chin with resignation. "But it can't. It won't. I won't let it."

"Right," Tika said and rolled her eyes. "You get yourself in the worst messes."

"I know," Sam admitted. "Trust me. I know."

THOUGH VICTOR WASN'T AS FANATICAL ABOUT SPORTS AS Javier and Conner, he usually enjoyed watching a game. Today, however, his mind continued to wander to the night before. Sam had been as delectable as he thought she'd be. Everything from the soft warmth of her skin to the sweet sounds she made as he'd loved her. She'd been damn near perfect.

He wished she hadn't been. Because if she'd been an awful lover, it would be much easier for him to do the right thing. If she hadn't been so damned easy on his eyes, looking away might be easier. But she was as close to perfect as he thought a woman could be.

Smart, sexy, beautiful, and amazing in bed? Yeah, she was too good to be true.

Even so, what had happened the night before couldn't happen again. He wouldn't let it. He couldn't let it. They were coworkers. To be more specific, he was her boss. He couldn't go around sleeping with his subordinates. Not only could it get him in trouble, but it could make things awkward around the office.

Javier and Conner were right about that. If things got awkward, Sam might quit. They needed her. Not just to add diversity to the team but because he could see how much potential she had as an investigator. She hadn't been utilized properly at HEARTS. Sam had already proven her worth, and he hadn't even given her a cyber case yet. She'd prove her worth just by helping with their existing cases. Once they had something for her to really sink her teeth into, he had no doubt that she was going to shine. She was going to bring something to the team that would put E.I. above the other PI offices in the area.

Holly Austin had missed out by keeping Sam behind the reception desk. Sam was damn smart and far too clever to be making copies. She had already impressed everyone at E.I. with her ability to dig into records and find exactly what was needed.

She deserved to be an investigator. And she deserved to have a boss who treated her like a part of the team. Not... prey...as Javier had called it. Damn it. He owed her an apology. A big one.

And a promise to behave better in the future.

However, if he were honest with himself, he had no idea how he would stand by such a promise. Now that he'd tasted her, quite literally, he couldn't imagine being able to resist tasting her again. He'd have to keep his distance when she was around. He'd have to make sure he didn't get close enough to smell that sweet scent coming off her skin or the heat that seemed to roll off her and pull him in. He'd have to resist those flirty looks and sexy smiles they'd started sharing from the word go. And that wasn't going to be easy.

The increased volume of a commercial break distracted him from his thoughts. Walking into the kitchen, he had just cracked open a beer when there was a knock at his door. Carrying the imported bottle with him, he peered through the peephole and cursed—partly with excitement and partly with dread.

Opening the door, he smiled at the woman standing there. If he didn't know better, he'd think he'd summoned her simply by thinking of her. Hell, maybe he had. If she were some kind of supernatural seductress, that would explain so much. Not only why he found her irresistible but why she seemed to be so perfect for him.

Leaning against the door, he gave her an easy smile,

already forgetting all the reasons why he shouldn't. "You didn't say goodbye before leaving."

"I had an appointment at my masseuse," she said smoothly.

He narrowed his eyes, not only gauging the truth in her words but trying to rid his mind of the images that instantly filled it. Hands covered in oil sliding over her calves, up her thighs, over that luscious curve of her ass. Higher and higher until... He sighed as he realized how much trouble he really was in with this woman.

"I go once a month with my best friend. It's our way of treating ourselves for being somewhat responsible adults."

Victor grinned. "Somewhat?"

"Well, I don't think anyone would say I'm fully responsible for my actions. Would you?"

"Not likely," he said softly, but he found that trait annoyingly adorable. Standing back, he opened the door all the way so she could come in. "It's nice that you get to spend that kind of time with your friend."

"It's very nice," she stated as she walked in. As he closed the door, Sam rolled her shoulders back and drew a breath.

Uh-oh. That was never a good sign coming from a woman, especially one he'd recently had passionate sex with. His amusement faded as he realized they were about to hash out what had been distracting him all damn day. While that was necessary, he wasn't sure he was prepared.

"About last night," she started.

Victor waved his hand. She might be a somewhat functional adult, but he was the responsible party here. Not only because he made the first move, but because of his role at E.I. He appreciated her opening the conversation, but he couldn't let her take the blame for what they'd done.

"Before you say anything else, let me." Putting his hand to his chest, he said, "I apologize, Sam. I crossed lines that I shouldn't have with you."

She seemed surprised. "I wouldn't...say that. I mean...we are two consenting adults. It's just..."

"You've only been with E.I. for a week and are still finding your footing, and that shouldn't have led you to my bed."

She nodded. "Right. Look, it's not that I don't find you attractive. Obviously, I do—"

"But it's unprofessional," he finished. "At least until we get to know each other better."

"Exactly," she said. She smiled. "Wow, I'm really glad you feel the same. I was so worried you'd be upset."

"I'm not. I promise."

"Good," she said. "Okay, in that case. I'm going to go and..."

She stopped speaking when he leaned to open the door for her and the distance between them closed. Little electric sparks seemed to dance around them.

Victor stepped back and gestured toward the door. "Okay. I'll see you Monday, then."

"See you Monday," she said. But she didn't move.

She was looking at him with uncertainty, but not because she was confused. She clearly wasn't confused. She was tempted. And so was he. Logic didn't seem so logical as he looked into her eyes. Common sense didn't matter nearly as much. All those reasons he'd been telling himself all morning no longer mattered.

What the hell was it about this woman that drove him so crazy he was willing to risk everything?

Before he could stop himself, he set his beer on the entryway table, gripped her hip, and pulled her to him. When their lips met, there was no tenderness in them. The kiss was crushing, full of longing and fantasizing and more than enough pent-up frustration.

Arching her back at the feel of his hands sliding up it, Sam kissed him harder, opening her mouth to his as her fingers dragged through his hair and their tongues began exploring each other.

He pulled her against him and lifted her. With her toes several inches off the floor, she had no control of where he took her, but she didn't really seem to care. She didn't protest as he took a step forward and pressed her against the wall. He almost wished she would because he didn't seem to have the power to stop himself.

All logic and reason were gone the moment his lips had touched hers. The only thing that mattered was that he extinguished the burning she had started deep inside him. Moaning when he dropped her to her feet, Sam rolled her head back, pushing his face into her neck while his hands roamed under her shirt and over the bare skin of her back and kneaded her bottom. Like his kisses, his hands seemed to be moving on their own, desperate and hungry for her.

Wrapping her leg around him, Sam pushed her pelvis to his, grinding against him, causing him to mutter something that even he couldn't make out. Victor wasn't sure if he actually spoke the words of encouragement that were screaming in his mind and throughout her body, but it only took a moment before she tugged at his shirt, and he felt a rush of cool air over the small of his back. That, combined with the sensation of his mouth tasting her neck, was almost too much. However, when Sam gasped and then dragged her nails over his skin, Victor lost what little control he had.

He cupped her breast, moaned her name, and was about to pull her from the wall and take her upstairs when she put her hands to his chest and pushed him back a step.

"I want you so much," she breathed, a hint of regret in her voice. "But we can't."

Slowly opening his eyes, he sighed. She was right. She was more than right. They couldn't do this. Shouldn't do this.

Cupping her face, he blew out a breath. "Sorry."

"Don't apologize," she said and then grinned. "It's good to know this is mutual."

"It's very mutual," he muttered.

Leaning in, she kissed him lightly on the lips. "Good. Then we both know that when we are ready, when we are in a better place, it will be worth it."

"It will be," he promised.

Pulling her from the wall, he hugged her tightly then steered her toward the door. "Don't come back here," he said teasingly, "until you're ready to finish this."

Sam laughed as she left his house.

"Hey," he called as she trotted down the stairs. She turned and looked up at him. "In case I didn't tell you, you were right to try to find the middle ground on this case. I might not have liked it, but you were right."

A beaming smile covered her lips. "Thank you."

"Now get out of here before I change my mind about doing the right thing."

He closed the door behind her and let out a long breath. Grabbing his beer off the table, he went back to the living room. The game was back on, but he gave up pretending to be interested in it and walked to the counter where he'd set the Carlton case documents. As he took a drink, he debated the next step. Not what it *should* be—obviously, they had to question Annette's father. What he was debating was how to confront the man who may have inadvertently been responsible for his daughter's death.

There was no way to prove that his debt was tied to what had happened to Annette, but Victor felt it in his gut, and his gut rarely led him astray.

Unless his beautiful new coworker happened to be involved.

Exhaling loudly, Victor rubbed his eyes. He had to get Sam out of his head. Every thought seemed to lead back to her. That set him on edge. He shouldn't be so enamored with her already.

He didn't know her well enough. And if he'd learned anything by being a PI, it was that this kind of fascination usually led to trouble one way or another. He doubted he'd end up in a cold case file somewhere down the road, but he had no doubt this situation was going to teach him a lesson he'd carry with him for a long time.

"Focus," he said, dropping down into a chair to look over the file. "How are you going to get this man to talk?"

He'd have to follow him. Learn his routine. Find the

perfect time to approach him. He should do that alone. Sitting in a car with Sam for days could prove too dangerous for both of them.

Cursing when he realized where his train of thought had gone again, he decided he needed to solve a completely different problem.

How to get Sam working on a different case so he didn't have a reason to keep thinking about her.

[5]

Monday morning came quickly, and with it, a shadow of shame clouded Sam. She walked into the E.I. office and smiled weakly at Lorraine and, instead of saying good morning to her coworkers, slithered into her office. She didn't think Victor was the kiss-and-tell type, but she didn't know. She'd told her best friend about their tryst, after all. What would stop Victor from telling his brother? Or his brother from telling his best friend?

She tried to convince herself this wasn't high school. Even if they had heard about the night Sam and Victor had shared, they wouldn't snicker and poke fun at her.

Would they?

No. They wouldn't. She was certain of it. Kind of.

Damn it. She certainly knew how to screw herself...no pun intended.

Her heart started to beat faster when she heard deep voices carrying through the hallway where the offices were located. Morning chatter had begun, and she couldn't help but fear it was about her.

"Hey, Sam," Conner said as he walked by her open door.

"Hey," she said, noticing how her voice was just a bit too high. Nervous. She'd sounded nervous. Normally, she wouldn't worry about someone noticing that, but she worked with a bunch of private investigators. They were always suspicious and looking for clues.

He hadn't missed it. He took a step back and poked his head in at her. "Everything okay?"

She smiled and nodded, doing her best to be cool and collected. "Not enough coffee yet. Is there any left in the break room?"

"Doubt it. Vic has been in for a while. He probably guzzled it by now."

She laughed lightly. "Well. I guess I'll make a fresh pot then."

He jerked his head to acknowledge her comment. "The morning meeting is in fifteen. See you there."

"Yup." She closed her eyes the moment he disappeared and silently cursed herself for being so weird.

She walked into the breakroom just as Javier finished filling his cup. "Oh good, there is coffee." That was better. She didn't sound so nervous when she said that. But then he looked at her and smiled, and that self-doubt hit her again.

He grabbed a cup and filled it for her. "What's Monday without a strong cup of coffee? Or ten." He laughed as he replaced the pot. "How was your weekend?"

She froze. "Fine. Yours?"

"Not too bad. See you in the meeting," he said and walked out of the breakroom.

Sam blew out her breath. She was being paranoid, that's all. Victor wouldn't dare tell their coworkers that they'd slept together.

She almost had herself convinced of that when it was time to join the meeting. She hadn't seen Victor yet this morning. He usually popped by, undressed her with his eyes, and then gave her a sexy smile before moving on. He hadn't done any of those things. Yet.

Don't be awkward, Sam told herself. *Don't be awkward.*

She carried her coffee cup into the conference room as the meeting was about to begin.

Though her coworkers were speaking, giving updates on their cases, Sam could hardly hear over the beating of her heart. She didn't know why she was acting so weird. So she'd slept with her boss. So they'd agreed they wouldn't do it again.

So she had been immensely disappointed when he hadn't stopped by her office and given her his usual seductive smile. Why would he? They'd agreed they weren't going to continue sleeping together. They'd agreed they weren't going to see each other again until they had a chance to know each other better.

So of course he'd stopped openly flirting with her. Of course he'd stopped looking at her like she was a forbidden treat.

Why the hell was she letting that get to her?

"Sam," Victor said.

She blinked and looked at him. "Huh?"

"I said that I found the most current address for Roger Carlton," Victor announced. "I'm going to follow him for a day or two before questioning him. I want to know what he's been up to before we tip him off that we're looking into Annette's murder. Just in case he does know something. Javier, can you ride with me?"

Sam creased her brow as she looked at Victor but swallowed down the urge to argue. Why would he bring Javier in on this case now? She stopped herself from asking. Maybe, like at HEARTS, the investigators here weaved in and out of cases. But it seemed wrong to her. Like Victor was being intentional about this decision.

"I need you to do some research, Sam," Victor explained after Javier agreed to be his partner for the stakeout.

Sam held her hand over her tablet, ready to peck on the touchscreen. "Of course. What should I be looking into?"

He shifted and she realized, probably right along with everyone else, that he was lying. Or so it seemed.

"I...um... I want you scouring that police report to look for more names and see if there are any other murders we can tie to this situation."

While that seemed logical, it also seemed like an excuse. She didn't think he'd sink so low as to avoid her after the night they'd shared, but then again...how would she know?

As soon as the meeting ended, Victor rushed out of the room. Another sign that things weren't as cool between them as he'd tried to tell her when she'd stopped by to tell him they couldn't be together right now.

Rather than accept his childish behavior, Sam carried her tablet as she casually strolled toward his office. She smiled when Javier nodded at her as she bypassed him. Stopping at Victor's door, watching him nervously shuffling through papers, she said, "Is there anything specific I should be looking into, or am I throwing spaghetti at the wall?"

He looked up, almost seeming embarrassed. "Spaghetti, I guess."

"Victor," she pressed.

He finally sighed and let his shoulders sag. "Give me a break," he whispered loudly. "I'm trying."

"Trying to what?" she asked in the same semi-hushed voice.

"Be normal."

She stared at him and then chuckled. "Really? Because you're doing a lousy job."

"I can't look at you without wanting to..."

He dragged his hand over his face, and her concerns faded. Poor guy. He wasn't avoiding her. He was horny. How sweet.

Sam grinned.

"I can't be in a car with you, Sam," he said. "I'm sorry. I just...I need you to stay here and work on looking for any other cases."

Her smile spread. "You are kind of being pathetic right now."

"I'm aware," he agreed.

"Fine. I'll stay here, but you had better not question him without me. I want to be with you when you question him."

Victor nodded. "I understand. Now...leave before I do something stupid."

She winked at him before walking out with her confidence renewed. Thank goodness he wasn't avoiding her out of regret. She didn't know how she'd take that. She couldn't exactly walk out of E.I. and never see him again. There was too much at stake for this case—for Holly's case, to be specific. Sam couldn't blow this opportunity to help her friend over sex.

Pulling the file she'd gotten from HEARTS closer, she started flipping through the pages, reading the information again. If they had found another case, she was certain they would have told her, but she wanted to confirm that she hadn't somehow missed a lead. Or a crumb. Or a clue.

Though she'd read over a hundred cases before, this was the first time she was doing so as an investigator, and she had to be meticulous. She couldn't let the smallest thing slip through. Though Holly didn't know it yet, there was progress being made on her mom's murder. Sam refused to be the reason that progress slowed or came to a halt.

Which led her back to her one-night stand with Victor. Though she was relieved that he hadn't been avoiding her, she might want to consider if it would be in her best interests to avoid him. He was a serious distraction. His dark eyes, his sweet smile, his scent... Everything about him made her mind go fuzzy. That was the last thing she needed right now.

She scoffed when she realized that her attention had faded once again. Tapping her forehead, she tried to physically force thoughts of that man from her head.

"Focus," she whispered.

With a firm shake, she whispered the words she was reading so her mind wouldn't wander quite so easily. Once she confirmed there was nothing in the notes about a possible case being tied to Tracy Austin's, Sam pushed the file aside and logged into her computer.

"Okay," she said, opening up a site with old police reports. "Let's see what we can find."

Grabbing a pen, she started writing out a list of keywords to search. She'd make her way through the list, checking them off as she went, until she found something. *Hopefully* found something.

She hoped this wasn't going to be a dead end. She needed something, just one more thing, to go on to figure out who had been behind these crimes.

"One case," she muttered before typing in the first keyword. "I just need one more case."

THE RUNDOWN NEIGHBORHOOD WHERE ROGER CARLTON lived looked like something out of a dystopian movie. Trash blew around the streets, and old, torn furniture littered overgrown yards. The houses seemed to barely be standing. One strong Midwestern storm would likely topple the entire neighborhood.

Victor parked along the curb several houses down from Roger's, fully aware that his sedan—while not the newest model—was going to stand out. Every other car on the block was rusted and dented. Settling in, he sipped his coffee and looked at the one-story shotgun shack with peeling yellow paint.

"What a freakin' dump," Javier muttered.

Victor flipped through his file. "He's been on disability for the last fifteen years."

"There are better places to live, even on the meager offerings of a disability payment. He's spending that money on something else. Guarantee it. Drugs?"

"Gambling. If I had to bet," he said and then grinned.

Javier moaned. "Dude, that sounded like something Dad would say."

Victor laughed, mostly because he couldn't argue. Their dad had the cheesiest sense of humor.

"You really think this guy ever leaves his house?"

Victor nodded toward the front door when it opened, and Roger Carlton shuffled down the sidewalk. "There he is."

Javier blew out his breath as they watched the man move in a way that was far too slow and labored for his age. The man looked like he'd had a rough life. Probably one of his own making.

They sat quietly watching him turn right when he left his property and headed toward the intersection. He lived just a few houses from a busy street with several rundown shops, liquor stores, and a bus stop. The type of intersection where a lot of bad business went down.

Victor wouldn't be the least bit surprised if Roger had made a deal or two there himself.

"Why am I here?" Javier finally asked. Looking at his brother as Roger continued to slowly move away from them, he cocked a brow. "Why did you tell Sam to stay at the office?"

Silence filled the car.

"Man, come on," Javier pressed. "You don't need me to help you watch this old guy. What's up?"

Victor still didn't say anything. He hadn't needed Javier, but it was a good excuse to not bring Sam. She'd known it was an excuse too. He saw it on her face. He had felt bad, but he'd meant what he told her. He couldn't possibly sit here next to her and keep his wits about him. He needed to keep an eye on Roger, not stare at her, remembering every kiss and touch and move they'd made together.

Javier moaned miserably. "Do not tell me that you slept with her. Already? Vic! What the fuck is wrong with you, man?"

He ground his teeth together. Damn it. He should have brought Conner. "I didn't mean to."

Javier snorted. "There are an awful lot of things that have to happen in order to have sex with someone. You have to find time alone. You have to agree to have sex. You have to get undressed. You have to—"

"Okay."

"I'm just saying there was time between getting her alone and getting her into bed where you could have stopped things."

"I know." He dragged his hand over his face. "I should have, but..."

"But you're a pig."

"But I'm a pig," he admitted. "I like her. I like her a lot, but I shouldn't have slept with her."

"A little late to figure that out now."

He watched Roger turn the corner. As slowly as the man

was moving, he wasn't concerned with losing him, so rather than pulling from the curb, he looked at his brother.

"If I didn't like her, I wouldn't feel like such a jerk, but I do like her. She's smart and sassy and beautiful."

"So what are you going to do?"

"I don't know. Nothing. I need to try to keep a respectable distance between us, which is why you're here. I need a clear head to figure out this case, but I also need some space between Sam and me so things can cool off a little."

"Man," Javier said on a dramatic sigh. "You're going to run her off."

"I'm not—"

"You run off every woman who gets too close to you. It's what you do."

Victor opened his mouth to disagree, but his brother was right. "I'm not running her off this time. I like her. A lot."

"So you said. But you've liked other women in the past, and where are they?" Javier shook his head as if he were disappointed in his older brother. "Get going before we lose him."

Starting the car, Victor rounded the corner and parked again. "A turtle couldn't lose this guy. You ever see anybody walk so slow?"

"Check out the way he's looking around. It's almost like he's scared."

"Or waiting for someone," Victor said as a man approached Roger.

The fear on the older man's face was obvious, even from some distance away. Javier raised the camera that had been sitting in his lap and started snapping photos.

"Can you tell what they are doing?" Victor asked. "They're huddled awfully close together. Drug deal, maybe?"

"Maybe," Javier said as he peered through the viewfinder on the camera. The telephoto lens would magnify the image for him, making it easier for him to tell what was going on. "Roger gave the guy an envelope, but I don't see him getting anything in return. Looks like the other guy is counting money." Javier snapped a few more photos and then scoffed. "He just put a few bills in his pocket."

Though Victor couldn't see that much detail without the telephoto lens his brother was looking through, he could tell enough that Roger was protesting the action. Until the other guy grabbed him by the lapel and jerked him close. A warning to keep his mouth shut, no doubt.

"This old guy isn't dangerous," Javier said. "If he had any fight in him, he would have used it. Should we question him?"

Victor shook his head as the younger man walked away and Roger sat at the sheltered bus stop. "No. I want to see if we can ID that guy first. Get a better feel for what's going on."

Javier snapped a few more photos before lowering the camera and looking at Victor. "Want to know the best part about having Sam on our team?"

Scoffing, Victor asked, "What?"

"Her specialty is cyber investigations. She knows all the nooks and crannies to search for people like this guy. She'll be able to figure out who that shithead is before we finish lunch. Which you're buying, by the way."

"Figures," Victor muttered. While he steered them toward a fast-food chain, Javier texted with Sam to let her know what they had, what they needed her to do, and to ask what she wanted for lunch...Victor's treat.

"I get it," Victor said after accepting several bags with burgers and fries inside. "We need Sam."

"Yes, we do. And you need to remember that before you get scared and chase her off."

"You keep saying that."

"Because that's your pattern, big bro."

Victor glanced at him, not appreciating his brother's approach. "I don't have a pattern."

Neither of them believed that, but Javier was too distracted by the french fries to challenge him. Victor frowned as he thought back on his love life. He wouldn't exactly say he'd had a string of women, but there were more than he had realized until just now.

They had never stayed around too long, though. And thanks to Javier's assessment, Victor had to consider that was his doing. He had always blamed his job. He was married to his work. He had too many things going on running a business to get distracted by a relationship.

He had...excuses. Lots and lots of excuses.

That didn't make him scared. That didn't mean he chased women away.

He just wasn't so great at committing. There was a difference, and he'd thank his smartass brother if he could recognize that. But he couldn't bring himself to say it. Mostly because he didn't think he'd want to hear what Javier had to say.

Instead, he frowned and said, "You'd better not be eating my fries."

Javier simply laughed and shoved more fried potatoes into his mouth.

Back at the office, they walked in and headed right for Sam's office. While Victor doled out food, Javier gave Sam the little memory card from the camera. With Javier in the room, Victor was able to control himself better, but he couldn't stop himself from thinking how adorable it was that Sam stuffed five fries in her mouth with one hand while typing with the other.

"This could take a few," she said around the mouthful.

Javier dropped into a chair across from her. "How did we get along without you?" he asked, and Victor clearly heard the point he was making.

Rather than tell his little brother to shut the hell up, he took a bite of his cheeseburger while Sam rambled on about websites and public access to this, that, and the other. But Victor knew...or at least strongly suspected...that Sam didn't use websites and public access to whatever to get her information. Her information was too confidential for public access, but he didn't want to know.

"Did you have any luck finding any other cases?" Victor asked.

"Not yet," she answered without looking at him. "I've come up with a long list of keywords to search." She grabbed a notebook and held it out to him. "Feel free to add to it if you think I missed something."

He scrolled through the words written in bubbly hand-writing. Damn, even her writing was adorable. How the hell could someone's handwriting be adorable? He skimmed the list, taking his time to consider each one, mostly because it was a nice distraction. "This is a good list. I'll think about it and let you know if I come up with anything to add."

He handed the notebook back to her, ignoring the heavy sigh from the man sitting next to him.

A few minutes later, Sam sat forward. She licked her lips and brushed her hands together as she focused on her screen. Turning her screen for Victor and Javier to see, she showed them what she had found—a police photo and a detailed record of his previous arrests.

"Meet Jason McDee," Sam said. "No stranger to the law, apparently. Petty theft, assault. Real nice guy." She pecked away on a different browser window and let out a soft laugh. "Employed by McCarthy Pay Advance." She typed the name of his employer into yet another window and sighed. "A locally owned paycheck advance operation, which is a nice way to say they are loan sharks. People get advances on paychecks, but the interest is so high, when they pay it off, they are already short on cash to get them to the next paycheck. So, what do they do? Take out another loan. And then another, and another, until they are in over their heads and can't possibly make up the difference. It's a racket."

"And what's a loan shark without a collector?" Victor asked.

Sam grabbed a few more fries and frowned at Victor. "Looks like old Roger didn't learn anything from his daughter's death after all. He's in debt way over his head. I don't know if this company sells debt like the last one seemed to, but he owes them. A lot."

Victor wiped his hands on a napkin and then tossed it into the empty bag. "Let's look into McCarthy Pay Advance. There might be a way to find out how much he owes now."

Sam made a note and shook her head sadly. "Annette got killed and his debt got wiped out. And he turned around and got himself right back into the thick of it. What a dumbass."

"If he has a soul, he'll feel so guilty about what happened to his daughter that he'll tell us everything," Javier said.

"Not that we can do anything about it now," Sam said, that frown pulling at her lips. "Annette is dead, and we have no leads on the man who killed her."

"Don't give up yet," Victor said gently. "We've barely scratched the surface of this case."

She focused on him and smiled softly. "I'm not giving up, I'm just... I'm disappointed in him. I don't know him, but I'm disappointed in him. He was given a second chance at a horrific price, and it looks like he blew it."

The trance Victor had found himself in by looking into her sorrowful eyes was broken when Javier noisily sucked at his empty cup, slurping up the remnants of his soda, and then shaking the ice and slurping again.

Looking at his brother, intent on warning him to stop, Victor's words stuck in his throat.

Javier had raised his brows and was giving his own silent warning.

Only then did Victor realize he'd all but forgotten his brother was in the room. Sam must have as well. She shifted and pulled her burger closer, focusing on the sandwich she hadn't taken a bite from yet.

"We'll leave you to your lunch," Victor said as he stood.

"Thanks for digging into this so quickly."

"You're welcome," she said and turned her attention to her screen as a blush settled over her cheeks.

Javier gathered the trash and thanked Sam as well. He followed Victor out of Sam's office, but he didn't turn and go to his own office. He followed Victor and closed the door behind him as they walked into Victor's office.

"Don't start," Victor warned.

"What the hell was that?" Javier asked, ignoring Victor's very clear instructions. "*Don't give up yet, Sam*," he said with an overly feminine voice and batting his eyes. He cocked his head and furrowed his brows. "Man, you were flirting with her right in front of me."

"I wasn't flirting—"

"What the hell would you call it?"

"I was offering her some reassurance."

Pointing a finger at his brother, Javier held his gaze with a hard stare. "You better watch your step with her. She's part of this team now. I'll kick your ass if you screw her over."

"I'm not—" He didn't get to finish his protest.

Javier turned on his heels and marched out.

Dropping into his desk chair, Victor exhaled his frustration. It wasn't only Javier that had him upset, though. He'd done exactly what he'd feared. He'd sat in Sam's office and had gotten lost in her and had forgotten everything else.

Rubbing his eyes, he moaned. Man. What the hell was it about her that had him tied up in such knots?

He didn't know, but he was going to have to figure it out. And soon. Before he blew this case, his chance with Sam— running her off like Javier insisted he was going to do.

[6]

Two DAYS LATER, Sam sat in Victor's car looking at the trashy house Victor said belonged to the man they had come to question. Looking at the overgrown grass, she imagined it to be a breeding ground for ticks and fleas. There were probably bedbugs and other mites on the torn sofa sitting in the yard. All of which were probably starved for human flesh. Just the idea of walking through that insect-infested gauntlet made her start to itch.

"I don't think we should go in there," she said, digging her nails into her scalp as she imagined lice crawling around his home, looking for a host.

"I agree a hundred and ten percent," Victor muttered. He shivered, and she figured he was having the same, or similar, visions dancing through his head.

Thankfully, they didn't have to go anywhere near Roger Carlton's home. Just as Victor had noted in the file he'd shared with her, Roger shuffled out of his house at ten o'clock on the dot and headed for the bus stop. He had done the same the previous two days. He was headed to a local casino. He'd sit at the slot machines for hours, drinking the free sodas and eating more than his share of the little bags of chips tucked at the refreshment stations while losing what little money he seemed to have.

As Sam had said a few days ago, he had blown the second chance he was given. The one Annette had died to give him. What a piece of shit. He'd had years to get help for his gambling addiction. He'd had years to turn his life around and make something of himself. Maybe even find a way to give back to others to make up for what had happened to his child, but instead, he was in the same cycle that undoubtedly had led to her death.

Roger sure didn't seem like he'd cleaned up his act much since his daughter's death all those years ago. In fact, Sam thought he probably hadn't cleaned up at all. Sam couldn't find an ounce of sympathy for him, even as he moved hunched over and clearly miserable to spend yet another day throwing away his money. She frowned as they climbed out of the car. For the first time, she was getting a better understanding as to why some of the HEARTS seemed so harsh at times. It was hard to feel sorry for someone who didn't seem to be trying very hard to make amends for past mistakes.

The smell of whiskey and cigarettes seemed to be coming from his pores as she leaned against the shelter of the bus stop. Standing this close to him, she thought he could pass for a homeless man. He hadn't bathed recently, and she didn't think he'd washed his clothing in weeks, if not longer. Her stomach turned at the stench and her anger toward him grew.

He didn't have to have a life like this. He didn't have to piss away everything he had. How disappointed Annette would have been if she could see him.

Victor was much braver than Sam and sat next to him.

"I paid this month," Roger said with a gravelly voice that spoke to how broken his soul seemed to be. His gray eyes were dull, probably from the alcohol in his system. His skin was so greasy, she could see the sheen on his T-zone. He looked completely broken, like he had nothing left to give to anyone.

Something inside of Sam almost released some of her anger at him and let a little pity slip in, but then she recalled the photos of the crime scene—the last images of Annette ever taken—and the kindness faded away and she reminded herself that he had a chance to turn things around.

Victor glanced up, giving Sam a knowing glance. Yup. The man hadn't changed a bit.

"We're not here to collect on our debt, Mr. Carlton," Victor said.

Roger finally stopped staring stoically ahead and turned his face to Victor. "Then what do you want?"

"We're private investigators," he said. "We look into cold cases."

Roger didn't reply. He was hard to read, but Sam was certain he must have been trying to figure out what that had to do with him. He was probably going back in time, thinking of all the petty—or not so petty—crimes he'd committed to feed his gambling habit. She had to wonder if he even registered that this could be about his murdered child.

"Right now," Victor said, about to spring it on the old man, "we are looking into your daughter's murder."

That got a reaction. Roger's eyes widened as he finally seemed to grasp why they were there. He sat taller, his back straightening for the first time since he'd walked out of his house. His mouth opened a few times, gaping as if he didn't know what to say.

"Why? Who hired you?"

"Nobody," Victor said. "I take on cases like this because everyone deserves justice. Even after all these years."

"So you just do this out of the good of your heart?" the man asked with a snide tone.

After a moment, Victor said, "My parents were killed when my brother and I were young."

Sam jerked her eyes to him. She hadn't known that about him. He'd never said. She was reminded how little they knew of each other. She wanted to hug him then, tell him how sorry she was for the loss that he'd suffered so long ago. A loss that seemed to still haunt him. She'd have to find a way to ask about that later, ask if he'd found their killer, if he'd managed to put his grief to rest.

"The police gave up on finding the killer. Crimes like that happened all the time in the area where we grew up. They didn't do much about it. But even if the cops thought that it wasn't a big deal, it was to me and my brother. I know how much it hurts to have unanswered questions. I try to do what I can for the families of these unsolved cases."

"Well, move on to the next one," Roger stated. "Nobody needs you looking into this."

Sam cocked a brow. "So you don't want to know who killed your daughter?"

Roger clenched his jaw and returned his gaze straight ahead. That movement convinced Sam that he already knew who had taken Annette's life. He didn't look guilty, though. Sam would have thought he'd feel guilty. He looked scared.

"We know about your debt," Victor said. "And how it was paid off soon after Annette's death. We know you owed some very bad people a lot of money."

Roger stood and started to walk away.

"Did she die to repay your loan?" Sam called. "Did your gambling addiction cost you your daughter?"

The man spun and glared. That was the most alert she'd seen him. He actually seemed to have genuine emotion in that moment. Anger lit in him, but she didn't think it was aimed at her. Though he was more alert, he didn't seem focused on her. He was looking through her, furious over something only he could see, a memory or his own guilt.

"I don't know what happened to her."

"She was raped and stabbed to death," Sam said. "That's what happened to her. And then your debt magically disappeared." She stepped closer, but not close enough to smell him. "Did you trade your daughter's life to get out of debt?"

Roger finally focused on her and creased his brow. "No. I loved my daughter. She was better than me. Better than I could ever dream of being."

"Yes, she was," Sam stated.

"I would have traded my life for hers. I still would."

"Who killed her?" Victor asked.

"I don't know. I don't know who they sent—" He stopped speaking abruptly.

Victor stood. "They who?"

Roger's spark faded as quickly as it appeared. He went from stiff and defensive back to slouched and defeated in the blink of an eye. With a shake of his head, he mumbled, "If you know so much, you don't need to ask me."

Sam wasn't about to let him off the hook that easily. She had absolutely no doubt that he was responsible for what had happened to Annette. She might not be able to hold him accountable in the eyes of the law, but she would be damned if she let him forget the ball he put in motion—what he had done to his own daughter.

"A neighbor says she saw a tall bald man outside Annette's house the night she died," Sam said. "Do know who he was?"

Roger stared and then smirked. "You think they'd use someone local to collect debt? Someone who could get caught? Someone people know? Collectors go in, do what they're told to do, and leave. I don't know who he was, and you'll never find him. They're like ghosts," he said quietly. "Do what they were hired to do and then...poof. Gone."

"And you think that's what happened to Annette?" Sam asked bitterly. "And you didn't think the police should know that?"

He simply stared at her, as if he didn't have a reasonable response. "I didn't trade her life for my debt. They *took* her life because of my debt. I wasn't given a choice."

"Of course you were. You could have paid off what you owed."

"There is no paying off. Don't you listen? You don't even know the kind of trouble you're in until you're in over your head. People like that don't tell you what the real price is."

"I'm guessing Annette knew. That's why she tried to cut you out of her life."

Roger lowered his eyes instead of answering.

"They killed her anyway. You coward," Sam spat.

Victor put his hand up in the way that Holly did when she wanted everyone to shut up. "Roger, who did you owe money to? Who would have done this?"

"You aren't listening," Roger said. "You don't get it."

"Get what?" Victor asked. He seemed to be losing his patience as well.

"It doesn't matter who I owed money to because the people who lend you the money are never the people behind the money. They create the debt for people you never see, never meet. You never really know who you are doing business with, and you'll never pay it off. You borrow ten thousand and they add interest and fees and whatever the hell they want because they do whatever the hell they want. In a matter of weeks, you owe twenty, in six months you owe forty. They don't tell you this when you need the cash, but they drop you in over your head, and there's no way out."

"Do you know who your debt was really owed to?"

"They don't exactly advertise it," Roger said. "These aren't the type of people with storefronts. They don't exist. Get it? You don't find them. *They* find *you*. And if they do, it's already too late. So stop asking questions. Before they find you."

Roger pushed his way around Victor and shuffled off.

Victor let him go that time. They had probably gotten more out of him than they could have asked for. He obviously was still indebted to whoever it was that was keeping him in gambling money. If he said too much, he'd end up dead too.

"Oh my God," Sam said when they were alone. "I wonder if Holly's dad had debt too. That would explain why she hasn't had a break in this case for so long. She probably wouldn't think to look into her own father. Holy shit."

Victor paused as he widened his eyes. "What?"

Sam immediately realized what she'd said. She had been so careful not to bring up Holly's name or Holly's case. She'd told him this was a random case that someone at HEARTS was looking into. She'd made it sound like she didn't know much. Right up until she'd blurted that out.

Damn it.

"I mean..." she tried, but a lie wouldn't form.

Victor let out a long slow breath. "Why in the hell would Holly need to look into her father?" he asked with a tense voice.

Busted.

VICTOR'S BREATH CAUGHT IN HIS CHEST, AND HE blinked, long and slow, as he waited for her response. She didn't seem to have one. While her deer-in-the-headlights look was usually endearing, at this moment, it infuriated him. This wasn't because she was flustered by his flirting. This lack of focus was because she couldn't seem to find a way around what she'd said.

"Samantha," he said as calmly as he could, "you need to answer me."

Her mouth opened. Closed. Opened again. But no words came from her perfect lips.

Rage filled Victor's veins as he started to fully process what she'd said. She'd all but admitted this wasn't a random case that someone at HEARTS had been looking into. This was personal to someone, apparently Holly, and rather than looping him into that, she'd lied. Repeatedly. To his face.

He'd known it! He'd known she was hiding something. Not only was she hiding something, but she'd clearly used his attraction for her against him. From the moment her eyes lit up in the meeting the other day, he'd suspected she wasn't being honest with him.

He was a damn fool. Just like his brother and Conner had said. And, of course, he hadn't realized how much of a fool he'd been until he'd slept with the little vixen.

"Don't," he warned when she started to speak.

"Vic—"

"Don't." Turning, he started to storm away, but she rushed around him. Narrowing his eyes when she put her hands to his chest, he glared. "I knew you were using me."

Her mouth fell open, and she widened her eyes. "What? I'm not using you!"

"Bullshit. I saw how your eyes lit when you heard about this case, and then you started sniffing around it like a stray dog."

Gasping, she took a step back. "A stray dog?"

"How would you describe it?"

Eyeing him like he was the most unappealing thing she'd ever seen, she said, "I wasn't sniffing, Victor. I was…"

He smirked when her words trailed off. "Yeah. Sniffing."

"There are similarities between a case I'm familiar with, but I haven't confirmed they are tied together."

"Something to do with your former boss."

She frowned. "I can't say."

"Well, you had better say something," he said, "because you're on thin ice with your current boss."

"I can't confirm that these cases are tied together…"

"Say something you haven't already said," he clarified.

"I'm working on it. Once I know…"

"Wrong," he stated. "Tell me what you know now."

Sadness, almost desperation, filled her eyes for a second, and he felt like a jerk but then remembered she was the one who had been keeping secrets.

"I can't say anything yet, Victor."

He exhaled loudly. "Get in the car," he said as he dug in his pocket. The car beeped as it unlocked.

"What? Where are we going?"

Turning, he stared at her. "We're going back to E.I., and you are going to get your shit out of my building. I don't want you working for me if you can't be honest with me."

The look in her eyes turned horrified. "What? You're firing me?"

"Yes." He walked around to the driver's side and climbed in. He started the ignition and waited. Finally, she climbed in. He expected her to spill the beans on what she'd been hiding, but instead, she crossed her arms and stared straight ahead.

Fine. She could have her way. Stubborn little shit.

Pulling from the curb, he drove away in silence. She sat, stiff as a board next to him, with clearly no intention of coming clean. The anger he felt grew tenfold. He was on the verge of exploding when he pulled into the parking lot. Before he even turned off the ignition, she hopped out.

By the time he entered the building, Lorraine had stood and was looking down the hallway.

"Ignore her," he muttered.

"What?" Lorraine asked, but Victor didn't stop to answer.

He went straight to his office, closing the door behind him. He looked around the space, but he was too angry to stay there. He opened the door and marched back out, right to Sam's office.

The space was still filled with her things, but she wasn't there. Probably looking for a box. Good.

He walked out into the lobby and looked at the receptionist.

"She said she'll be back for her things when you aren't here," Lorraine said.

Victor opened his mouth but decided he didn't have to explain himself. Lorraine cocked a brow at him and returned her focus to her computer screen. Walking to the glass door, he looked out just as she drove out of the parking lot.

Turning, he faced Lorraine and stared down her judgmental look. "She lied to me."

"About what?"

"Why she was interested in this case I'm working on."

"Okay," Lorraine said with a know-it-all tone. "Why is she interested in this case you're working on?"

"She says she can't tell me until she knows more."

"Sounds more like she's being careful than lying."

Victor huffed. Of course Lorraine would take Sam's side. He gave his head a firm shake. "She lied," he said as he started toward his office. "And I don't take kindly to being lied to."

He slammed his door, shutting out whatever it was that Lorraine was muttering under her breath. He didn't want to hear her thoughts on the matter. He didn't want to hear anything. Other than the truth from Sam.

[7]

Sam parked in front of Holly's house. She didn't know why she was there, but she was drawn. Moth to a flame or whatever the saying was. Slamming her head back against the headrest, she let out a long breath, and her eyes welled with tears.

She jolted when someone knocked on the passenger window of her car, but she didn't have to look. It was Holly. She wouldn't have missed Sam parking in front of her house. Sam considered her options for about three seconds before unlocking the doors.

"What are you doing here?" Holly asked, slipping into the passenger seat. She sounded angry and Sam couldn't blame her. Parking in front of her house like a pathetic stalker wasn't the best way to win someone like Holly over.

Sam sniffled and dragged her hands under her eyes. "I'm sorry." Her voice came out as a hoarse whisper. "I was afraid to call."

The air in the car changed. For the first time since their

big fight, Sam felt that familiar sense of Holly's protective side.

"What happened?" Holly asked. The hard edge in her tone wasn't directed at Sam. Holly was a mama bear if there ever was one. It wasn't like Sam to do this. To show up like this. To cry for no good reason. Holly knew something was wrong, and she immediately went on the defense.

That was something at least. Sam didn't think Holly would be ready to jump in and protect someone she hated as much as Sam thought she must hate her.

"I screwed up." Sam closed her eyes and swallowed hard. "I always screw up. I don't know why. You're right about me. I'm too self-centered."

"Sam?" Holly pressed. "*What* happened?"

"I got fired," she said and then sobbed. "We had sex the other night, and then he fired me this morning. It's not like I didn't see this coming. He's been flirting with me since I started. I just... I thought we'd at least have more than one night before he dumped me like this. I'm such an idiot. Oh no." She gasped and looked at Holly with wide eyes. "Do you think he dumped me because I'm bad in bed?"

Holly let out a breath as she closed her eyes. A few seconds later, she eyed Sam with that familiar you-drive-me-nuts look.

"Let's focus on the important thing here."

"I think that's important," Sam muttered before sniffling.

"Victor Estrada had sex with you, and then he fired you for it?" Holly asked with a razor-sharp edge to her tone.

The anger on Holly's face was plain to see, and while Sam would have loved to have basked in having her former friend rage on her behalf, she couldn't lie. Not to herself and certainly not to Holly.

Sam shook her head. "No," she said softly. "He fired me because I lied. Not lied...just...didn't tell him everything." Another sob choked from her. "Okay, so that's kind of a lie, but it was just because I was trying to protect you. If he knew you were my source, he'd come over questioning you and..." She closed her eyes as she realized she'd done it again. She'd opened her mouth and said way more than she should. "Oh, damn it."

More tears filled her eyes and fell down her cheeks when she realized that once again, she'd walked right into the mess she'd created.

"Protect me from what?" Holly asked.

Sam looked at her and tried to stop herself from crying, but she couldn't. She'd been bottling up so much of this stress and heartache. Ever since she'd been fired from HEARTS, she had been a wreck. She'd just hidden it well. Now the dam had cracked, and the waterworks wouldn't stop. The heaviness in her chest was more than she could bear. If she didn't let it loose soon, it might crush her.

She didn't even try to stop herself from sobbing this time. She leaned forward, put her head on her fur-covered steering wheel, and let it go. Minutes seemed to pass before Holly took a napkin from the glovebox and shoved it under Sam's nose.

"That's enough," Holly said gently but firmly. "Get your shit together, Sam. This is too much."

Sitting back, she wiped her cheeks and then her nose with the rough paper napkin. Her sinuses were full, but she didn't dare try to blow her nose into the harsh paper. She sniffled and huffed a few times instead.

"Talk to me," Holly insisted. "What's really going on?"

Sam licked her lip and scanned Holly's yard, looking at everything but her friend. "Victor is working a case." Her voice trembled as she spoke—partly from her emotional breakdown and partly because she knew the words she had to say were going to hurt Holly. The last thing she wanted in the world was to hurt Holly, but there was no easy way to break this to her. "Her name was Annette Carlton. She was raped and murdered in her home," she said softly. "In December 1989."

The blood drained from Holly's face. "When in December?" she whispered.

"On the eighth."

"Oh my God."

Sam nodded. "I saw photos of the crime scene. It... I think it could be the same man who killed your mom, but I can't prove it. Not yet anyway. One of Annette's neighbors saw someone. The description fit the guy you've been looking for. But the police... From what I can tell, they didn't look into him. They didn't seem very concerned about what happened to her at all. At least not from what I've seen of the police report. She came from a troubled home, and it seemed like they just wrote it off as if she deserved what happened to her. I wormed my way into Victor's case so I could learn what he knew in case..."

Emotion clogged her throat again. Even though she knew Holly was put off by these types of breakdowns, Sam couldn't stop herself. She managed to swallow down the sob filling her chest and wiped her eyes again. "If it's the same guy, I wanted to... I didn't want to tell Victor about your mom until I knew. But I slipped up and said your name. He figured out that I wasn't telling him everything and demanded to know what you had to do with his case. I wouldn't tell him, so he fired me."

Holly lowered her face and blew out a breath. "You're rambling, Samantha," she said softly.

Usually, a statement like that would be made with a roll of Holly's eyes before she marched off. But now, her eyes were downcast, her voice was quiet, and she was sitting still as a statue.

"I needed more information before I came to you," Sam said, hoping Holly understood. "I didn't want to give you a lead that might have been another dead end."

Finally, Holly lifted her face and offered a weak smile. "Thank you. I appreciate you looking out for me."

"You're welcome."

"I'm sorry Victor fired you."

Sam shrugged. "You would have fired me too. Wouldn't you? If I refused to give you information that could help solve a case."

"Probably. But I wouldn't have had sex with you first."

After a few seconds, Sam smiled and laughed lightly.

The light moment passed quickly. Holly looked around her before staring straight ahead. "What have you learned?"

"Not much yet, but we have a new direction to look. I'd like to investigate a bit more before sharing, if that's okay. I don't want to... You don't need to worry about this right now.

Let me look into it more. If I need help, I'll ask someone at HEARTS."

Holly looked out the window. "I appreciate you not dragging me into Victor's case without discussing it with me first. But I also understand why he was upset."

Sam lowered her face. "I know. I do too."

"But sleeping with his employee and then firing her? That's... Not cool."

"Well, to be fair," Sam said with a heavy sigh, "I didn't exactly shoot down his advances."

"You're the subordinate," Holly said with her usually stern tone. "It was his job to set the boundaries."

"*Was* the subordinate." She laughed flatly. "I've been fired twice in as many months. I'm such a fucking loser."

"You're not."

"I am."

"You could... You could learn a thing or two about boundaries too."

"Yeah. I'm working on it." She offered Holly a soft smile. "I realize now how much I overstepped with your wedding plans. I was taking over your day and making it my own. That was wrong and insensitive and...such a *me* thing to do. I'm sorry, Holly. I didn't mean to ruin your wedding."

"You didn't," Holly said, looking at her. "You didn't ruin anything. I shouldn't have lost my cool like that. I..." Turning her face away, she shrugged. "I know Jack and his mom want more than a courthouse wedding. I know they were disappointed when I said I didn't want to make a big deal about getting married, but they didn't push. I think the reason I kept putting off setting a date is because I didn't want to disappoint them, but I didn't know how to have a nice, quiet wedding that would be what everyone wanted. So... So I put it in your hands knowing it would be a disaster." Scoffing, she looked at Sam. "I knew you would get out of hand and I would get upset. I think on some level, I wanted you to screw this up so I could have an excuse to say I tried to have a real wedding and appease my guilt for not wanting one. I'm sorry, Sam. I made this mess and then blamed you for it."

Sam considered Holly's words for a moment. "No. I knew you'd hate what I was planning. I just got caught up. I overstepped."

"We both did. Let's put it behind us, okay?"

"Gladly."

"What are you going to do about your job?"

Sam shrugged. "I don't know."

"Do you want to stay at Estrada?"

"No. Things will be super awkward now."

Holly was quiet for a moment. "Were you expecting a relationship with him, or did you know this was a fling?"

Sam blew out her breath. "Both, I think. If I were honest. I wanted a relationship with him, and I thought he felt the same, but...clearly he didn't."

"Come back to HEARTS."

Shock rolled through Sam. She hadn't come here to get her old job back. Or expected to. "But...you hired Susan."

Holly chuckled. "Yeah. I did. To be our administrative assistant and office manager and...office mom. She's really good at that kind of thing. You? You're really good at that cyber stuff you're always doing for us. You should be our cyber expert. I haven't quite figured out where your office will be. We're getting cramped for space in that building, but you should have one."

Sam swallowed hard. If she let out the squeal building in her chest, Holly might change her mind. But she couldn't stop the smile that spread across her face. "We could get rid of the file room if you'd let me digitize everything like I've been telling you we should."

Holly seemed to consider that option before sighing. "Or we could get a storage unit for the paper files."

"You're such a hoarder."

"Paper files are still important."

"Whatever," Sam said, and her smile softened. "Thank you."

Holly nodded. "Are you okay?"

"I will be."

"So maybe... You can't *plan* my wedding, but maybe you could *help me* plan my wedding."

That was it. That was the last bit of good that Sam could handle. The squeal erupted and she clapped her hands. "Yes!"

Holly laughed softly and shook her head. "I've missed you, Sam. And I'm glad you're back." She climbed out of the car before Sam could respond.

Sam didn't mind. Holly didn't do girly emotions and excitement. This was about as much bonding as Sam could have expected out of her former boss... No, just boss. Holly was her boss again, and Sam was thrilled.

To hell with Victor Estrada. To hell with his handsome face and cocky smile.

Who the hell needed him anyway?

Victor wasn't in the mood to defend himself, but as he looked from Javier to Conner, he realized they didn't understand why he'd fired Sam.

"You did what?" Javier demanded as he stared at his brother.

Conner turned off the television he'd muted when Victor had arrived. Apparently, for once, something was more important than the game they'd been watching. "Are you fucking stupid?" he asked his boss.

"She lied."

"She didn't give you all the information."

"Which is lying," Victor said.

"Which means she was protecting someone's privacy until she had to give up that person's identity," Javier stated. "We do that shit all the time."

"This is different."

"Why?" Conner asked.

Javier scoffed. "Because he's using it as a reason to run her off. Like we knew he would."

Conner simply stared at Victor.

"I am not. She—"

"Fix it," Conner said, reaching for the remote.

Victor looked at his brother.

"Fix it," Javier repeated.

Victor sat looking between them for several more seconds before standing. "It's my company."

"Fix it," his employees said in unison.

With a huff, Victor turned and marched out of Conner's

house to leave them to their stupid game. Driving off faster than was logical in the neighborhood, Victor headed toward the office. He wasn't going to apologize. Not when Sam was the one who had kept pertinent information from him.

She was the one who hadn't been honest.

But as he drove, he replayed Javier's words. His brother had been right. They often retracted the name of a client or witness if the information wasn't necessary or the person might want privacy. He could understand why Holly would want privacy if someone she knew had been victimized the way Annette had been.

If Sam was wondering if Holly's dad was involved, it must have been her mother or maybe an older sister. Someone close enough that Holly was still looking into the crime.

That definitely explained why Sam was trying to protect her until she knew for certain there was something to tell.

Shit. He had overreacted. And Javier was right about something else. He'd done it because Sam was getting to him, and whether he wanted to admit it or not, he chased women off when they got too close.

God, he hated it when Javier was right.

Victor's gut twisted when he saw Sam's car in the parking lot. Since the front door was activated by a swipe of a card, everyone had access to the building, but he didn't think she'd be there. He thought about leaving, but he needed to settle this.

Ever since their confrontation earlier in the day, he'd felt queasy. He had likely overreacted, and that wasn't like him. Everything about his behavior when Sam was around was off. She had a way of making him feel unsettled, and he didn't like that. He didn't always think before responding because he always felt like he was in a freefall around her.

He owed her an apology for the way he'd reacted. He took a deep breath, manned up, and walked into the office to deliver it.

Leaning in her doorway, he watched her gather the few items she'd added to her office. "I didn't mean to snap," he said, causing her to jump.

She put her hand to her chest and cursed under her breath. "Don't do that. Damn it."

"Sorry," he said and smiled. She was adorable, even when she was mad at him. "I'd like to apologize. If you'll let me."

She simply looked at him as she eased a photo frame into a box.

"I had suspected there was more to your interest in my case. When you confirmed it, I reacted badly. For that I am sorry."

"And what would you have done if I'd told you the case I recognized was Holly's mom?"

Victor gawked at her. "I would have gone and talked to her."

"Exactly." Sam looked as frustrated as Victor felt. "You would have gone to Holly asking questions about something that is incredibly traumatic for her."

"I need to know—"

"And I need to protect my friend." Sam shook her head at him. "I wasn't trying to get something by you so I could somehow come out ahead, Victor. I wanted to get as much information as possible and break it to her gently. My God, she watched her mother get raped and murdered. Do you really think she'd be okay with you just marching in there and asking her to compare notes? That's not a conversation she's going to want to have with someone she doesn't know. She has to live with that trauma every day of her life." Sam frowned at him, and her usually bright eyes looked incredibly sad. "I was protecting her."

Man, he felt like an asshat. "I get that," he said gently. "But you weren't honest with me. If you'd just told me—"

"If I'd told you, you would have pressured me to tell you everything. Don't deny that."

He scoffed. He couldn't. He would have done just that, he would have pushed and pushed until she told him what he wanted to know. Looking at the box on her desk, he sighed. "Don't pack. I don't want you to go."

Sam didn't have the happy reaction he was expecting. If possible, she looked even more sad as she tilted her head. "Holly offered to let me go back to HEARTS."

"You don't want to do that, Sam."

"Actually, I do."

His heart dropped to the pit of his stomach. "You're going to give up an investigator position to go back to being their errand girl."

"I was never their errand girl," she stated firmly. "I was a part of their team, but now I'll get to be an investigator too."

He blew out his breath. "You're an investigator here."

"I've been here like two weeks, Victor, and you've already slept with me and fired me, so..." She emphasized her point by closing the box and lifting it off the desk.

"Those two things were not related, and you know it."

She started for the door but stopped in front of him and blew out a long breath. "I do think Holly's mom and Annette were murdered by the same man. And I do think you can find him. I'll help if I can."

"Sam," he said gently. "Can we talk about us?"

"There is no us, Victor. There was flirting and one really nice night, but there's no us."

He wanted to challenge her, but she left him standing there looking like the damned fool that he was.

[8]

Walking into HEARTS the next day and not stopping to work at the reception desk was weird. Good weird, but still weird. Unlike the last time she walked into this office, she didn't feel like a misfit sneaking around. She belonged here again. This was her home away from home again. That was nice.

"Oh my God," Alexa nearly screamed when Sam poked her head into her office. "It's about time you two straightened your shit out."

Sam laughed and walked into the office, setting her box on the chair next to her and easing her laptop bag off her shoulder.

"It was like two weeks."

"Two weeks too long."

"I need an office. We're going to have to move all those boxes from the storage room into actual storage because Holly won't part with them."

Alexa grinned. "Oh, you silly girl. It's already taken

care of."

Sam widened her eyes. "What?"

"Jack rounded up the menfolk, and they came in here last night and cleared out that room. They even put a desk in there for you."

Warmth filled Sam's heart. "Really?"

"We missed you, Sam. All of us. And we're very glad you're back."

"So am I," she said. She left Alexa's doorway and walked to the storage room that sat off the conference room. She was a bit isolated on the other side of the building from where the other offices were, but she had an office. Her own office. She really was an investigator now. She wasn't going to count the two weeks she'd spent at E.I. That was a mistake she was going to do her best to forget.

Sam carried the box she'd packed at her office at E.I. the other day right to the space she'd call hers. This time at HEARTS, where she belonged.

She suspected Holly picked out the furniture. Sensible. Plain. Practical. Yes, this was very Holly. The other ladies would have stepped things up a bit.

Sam didn't mind. She'd spruce things up soon.

Honestly, she was just happy to be back in this place, with her people. As soon as she unpacked the box, she cut the tape and flattened it to take out to the recycling bin. She was walking back inside when the front door opened.

Sam's excitement at being back at HEARTS fizzled when Victor Estrada walked in the front door.

"What are you doing here?" she demanded.

"I invited him," Holly said, coming in from behind Sam.

She had a file in her hands and walked straight to the conference room. At the door, she stopped and cocked a brow. "Get in here. Both of you."

Victor gestured for Sam to go first. She hesitated for a few seconds before following Holly into the room and taking a seat at the long oval table. The table was big enough to seat all of the HEARTS, and now Susan, but it still felt too small when Sam tried to determine where to sit so Victor wasn't too close.

Holly sat with a stiff posture and an unreadable look on her face. Oh shit. Sam hated that posture and that look. This meant Holly was about to lay down the law.

"I've been looking for the man who murdered my mother for most of my life," Holly stated. "I'll do just about anything to find him." She turned her hard gaze to Victor. "Sam thinks the case you're working on could be related."

"She said there are similarities," he said.

She blinked. That was the only sign she gave that the information impacted her. Victor probably hadn't noticed, but Sam had. She knew Holly well enough to know that blink was the equivalent of receiving a gut punch. Sam wanted to comfort her friend but knew better.

"I think it would be beneficial for us to work together to investigate. Don't you?"

Victor nodded once.

"I'm too close to this. I've realized that over time. I think the reason I haven't found whoever did this is because I'm too emotionally invested to see the evidence for what it is." She held up the folder she'd brought with her. "I'm willing to share information for information. On one condition," she stated and flicked her eyes toward Sam.

Sam sank back. Oh no.

"A member of my team will be involved in your investigation. And that won't be me. I won't be objective enough to help you. Everyone else is working cases already. That means you two will work together. Can you do that?"

Holly might have been staring at Victor, but once again, Sam knew her well enough to know she was giving Sam an out. Part of her wanted to back out, to say she couldn't work with this man. But she couldn't let Holly down. Even if she had to suck up working with the biggest jerk she'd ever met.

EVERYTHING VICTOR HAD HEARD ABOUT HOLLY AUSTIN was proving to be true. Even from across the table, and despite the fight they'd had, he could read the silent warning in Holly's eyes. He'd hurt Sam once. Holly was making it clear without a single word that he'd better not do it again.

"I trust," Holly said coolly, "that you can work together to find out what happened to my mother and..." She turned her gaze to Sam.

"Annette Carlton," Sam offered.

"Annette Carlton," Holly repeated with a softness that didn't seem to suit her stiff-as-a-board posture. "Have you looked for other similar cases? If I missed Annette's case, I could have missed others."

"I don't think you missed it," Victor offered. "I think the

reports weren't clear enough for you to make the connections."

"I appreciate that, but the fact is I'm too close to this. Alexa and Rene have been telling me that for a year. I just couldn't see the truth. They were right. I can't find my mother's murderer. But I'm trusting that you two can."

"We will," Sam promised.

For the first time, Victor realized the bond between them was strong. Sam had been fired, and he assumed that severed the ties that bound them. Clearly, he'd been wrong. Sam had a soft spot for this woman, and the feeling was mutual, though Holly seemed to hide it better.

Victor nodded his agreement. "We won't stop until we do."

"Thank you," Holly said. Standing, she slid the file across the table so it rested between Victor and Sam in a nice neutral spot. "This is a copy of my notes from what I remember about that night to all the research and dead ends I've hit. There might be something in there that helps."

Sam offered Holly a soft smile. "I have a copy already. Victor can have this one."

Holly didn't seem surprised.

Sam cleared her throat. "Holly... Did your parents owe money to anyone? Your dad... He drinks a lot, but does he gamble? Or..."

Holly took a breath and seemed to think about this for a moment before shaking her head. "Not that I know of. Why?"

Sam couldn't seem to come up with an answer, and Victor realized she was trying to protect her friend.

"It looked like Annette's father owed some ugly people money. We don't know if that's why she was attacked, but it is something we're looking into. If your parents owed money, it could be the link we're missing."

Holly stiffened. "I never looked into my parents' finances." A hint of a smile found her lips as she looked at Sam. "Again, I'm too close. You should look into that. I'll get you my dad's number and address in case you need to talk to him."

"Thanks," Sam said softly.

Holly simply nodded and left them alone.

"She's nicer than I expected," Victor said.

"For now." Sam turned and cocked a brow at him. "She'll tear you to shreds if need be."

He started to grin but suppressed it. That was a warning, and he wasn't going to dismiss it that easily. "Understood. I think we should start by looking for more victims that might be tied to this."

"I'm going to start there," Sam said. "I think you should try to figure out what Annette Carlton and Tracy Austin had in common. It's not their looks. Holly is the spitting image of her mother—blond, blue-eyed, tall. Annette had dark hair, dark eyes, and was average height."

Victor nodded with realization. "That was why you wanted to see my case file that day in the meeting."

Sam shrugged. "Usually, serial rapists have a type. If Annette had looked like Tracy, it would have been easier to explain the motive, but right now, we don't know why this man would target two different women who seemingly had nothing in common."

"We don't know that it was the same man."

As she lowered her eyes, she drew a deep breath. "It's the same man. I feel it in my gut."

"Okay. I'm going to start digging into anything I can find to tie them together." He took the file off the table as he stood. "We'll touch base at the end of the day."

Sam nodded. For the first time since he'd met her, there were no flirty gazes or lusty undercurrents between them. For the first time, he felt awkward around her. After blowing out a slow breath, he rolled his shoulders back, readying himself to own up to his actions.

"I was out of line with you, Sam."

"Which time?" she asked, standing up to face him.

That was fair. "Every time I knowingly led you to believe I wanted more than a working relationship. I did," he quickly clarified. "But I was out of line to be so open about it. And I was definitely out of line to—"

"Have sex with me when you were my boss?"

"Yes," he said as he felt heat settling over his cheeks.

Sam tilted her head in a way that led him to believe she was about to read him the riot act, but then she smiled. "I'm sorry too. I had intended my time at E.I. to be a fresh start, but I just did what I always do. Screw things up. Literally this time," she added with a mutter and half grin.

"Sam, I—"

"We both were out of line. Let's just wipe the slate clean, okay? Please," she added, and her cheeks turned as red as he imagined his were. "I'd really like to just...forget I jumped your bones within a month of working with you. I think I was in a bit of an emotional death spiral from my fight with Holly, and you were a nice distraction."

Victor inhaled sharply at the shock of her confession. Not because he was surprised but because she was so honest about it. "Ouch."

She chuckled. "Oh, please, Victor. Don't tell me you fell in love the moment you saw me."

He started to tell her he fell into something, but she was right. It wasn't love, and he wasn't foolish enough to think it was. However, he did feel something for her. He felt some kind of inexplicable connection.

"Lust," he said. "I fell in lust."

"Yeah," she said warmly. "Me too. But now... Well, maybe someday...but for now, we are working this case. Nothing is more important to me right now than solving this case so Holly can put the past to rest. She deserves that."

Victor took that as his cue to wrap this up. "I agree. I'll head back to my office and see what I can dig up that might connect them."

"And I'll start looking for more victims."

He started for the door but then stopped. "Once we solve this, I'd like to take you to dinner."

"Like a date?" she asked.

"Yeah. Like a date. Fresh slate and all."

Smiling in a sweet way, she said, "We'll see."

[9]

Daniel Austin didn't seem to be getting along much better than Roger Carlton.

Sam had only met Holly's dad once—some time ago when Holly had been hurt on a case, he'd sobered up for about five minutes. He'd come and taken her to lunch one day. That had been some time ago.

As he opened the door to his tiny house now, he looked rugged as hell. His bloodshot eyes settled on Sam and then looked beyond her to Victor.

"Hey," Daniel said in a grainy voice that reminded Sam of a washed-up lounge singer.

She smiled anyway. "Hi, Mr. Austin. Remember me?"

"Vaguely," he said.

"I work—"

"With Holly," he finished. "I remember."

She gestured behind her, "This is Victor Estrada. He's a private investigator too but with a different firm. We're working together on some cases that have some evidence in common. I was hoping we could ask you a few questions."

"About?"

Sam hesitated. "You know that Holly has been trying to solve her mother's murder."

He didn't reply, but he did flinch. He jolted and blinked as if he'd been slapped. Finally, he said, "I've told her to let that go. Her mother died a long time ago. Nothing can come of digging up ghosts now."

Sam offered him a soft smile. "I don't think Holly sees it that way, Mr. Austin. She's still quite traumatized by what she witnessed that night."

"That's even more reason to let it go. All she's doing is reliving a damn nightmare instead of letting herself wake up and move on."

Watching him squeeze his hands into fists and grind his teeth so hard the muscles in his jaw flexed, she had to wonder if he'd always had this reaction to the mention of the night Tracy Austin died, or if he was upset that Sam and Victor were bringing it up.

She glanced toward Victor, and he seemed tense as well, as if he were ready to pounce on Daniel if needed.

"The thing is," Sam said as gently as possible, "Holly's never going to be able to let go and move on until she feels justice has been served. She watched her mother die, Mr. Austin. She's not going to simply let that go."

"It was a long time ago," he stated firmly. "Too damn long ago to serve up any kind of justice now."

"Well, Holly would like to try, and we are trying to help her."

This time, his only reply was a heavy sigh and a shake of his head.

"It's very important to her," Sam pressed.

"It was a long time ago. There's nothing to solve. Not anymore."

"That might not be accurate," Victor offered. "There seems to be new evidence. If you can give us a few minutes of your time, we'll explain."

Daniel hesitantly let them in. Sam put her hand under her nose as she stepped inside. The smell of musty carpet and stale beer nearly knocked her off her feet. She only needed a moment to acclimate, though, and she was able to fake a smile as she did her best to ignore the mess around her.

God. No wonder Holly had told Sam questioning her dad was probably pointless. The man could barely take care of himself, let alone answer questions about a crime that had happened so very long ago.

Daniel scooted around, grabbing up empty cans and food containers. "I wasn't expecting company," he muttered.

"It's okay," Victor assured him. "We'll only be here a few minutes."

"I don't know what else I can tell you," Daniel said, depositing his overflowing load of trash near a small can that didn't have any room left in it. "I've told Holly everything I can about that night. I've told her a thousand times."

"We found a case that was similar to the night your wife died," Sam said softly. "In that case, a neighbor saw a man who seemed to fit the description Holly gave to the police. That's enough for us to believe it was the same man."

Daniel stood up and looked at her. If he were sober, she

might have been able to read his eyes, but he was bleary and swayed as he stood before her.

"We were able to determine that in that case," Victor said, "the victim's father owed money to a loan shark. What's more, it looks like that loan shark sold off the debt to... Let's say, someone even less on the up and up."

Daniel shook his head and started gathering more empty containers. "I wouldn't know about that. I don't know who you're talking about or what you're talking about. Tracy died a long time ago." He carelessly tossed the trash he'd gathered aside and looked at Victor. "Holly isn't the only one who was traumatized by that night, you know. I came home and found Tracy dead on the floor and Holly practically catatonic. I was traumatized too, damn it. I don't know anything about a loan shark or whoever else you're talking about. I don't know anything."

Sam glanced at Victor, and they seemed to share the same thought—they didn't believe him. "We're not trying to upset you," she said gently.

"Well, you *are* upsetting me. Does Holly know you're here?"

"Yes," Sam stated firmly. "Yes, she does. She wants to get to the bottom of this. At all costs," Sam added.

"Mr. Austin," Victor said, stepping closer to Daniel, "did you or your wife owe money to anyone?"

"We're not judging," Sam was quick to say. "We honestly just want to help Holly find some peace."

Daniel stopped glaring at Victor long enough to eye Sam. "You want to help Holly? Then you convince her to let this go. You convince her that there is no solving this case and she needs to let it go. Because she damn well won't listen to me, even when it's for her own good." He pointed a crooked and dirty finger at Sam. "You tell her no good can come from digging up the past over and over. You tell her that Tracy is dead and buried, and we need to let her rest now. Holly needs to accept that her mother is gone and let it go."

"That might be easier if she hadn't seen her die," Sam said softly.

Something like guilt seemed to fill his drunken eyes. Shaking his head, he muttered to himself and shuffled to a torn recliner. Dropping down, he stared into space, as if he could ignore what she'd said.

Moving closer, Sam did her best to play on what little paternal instinct the man might have possessed under all that booze. "Holly's getting married soon. She's about to start a new life with Jack. She really wants to be able to do that without those horrific memories haunting her."

Daniel looked at Sam. "Knowing who's to blame doesn't change what was done."

"No, it doesn't," Sam said. "But it might make the burden easier to carry."

"We don't need names from you," Victor offered. "We just need to know if you owed someone something. Something significant enough for them to try to collect on it."

Panic seemed to fill Daniel's eyes. They were getting close to the truth. Sam could smell it... Well, she could smell *something*.

"Please," Sam whispered. "For Holly. Tell us the truth for Holly."

Daniel let his eyes swim again, smacked his lips a few

times, and then said, "I don't know why anyone would kill Holly's mom. She was a good woman. She loved our little girl more than anything. Holly loved her too. They were two of a kind. Peas in a pod. I know it hurt Holly to see what happened that night." He swallowed hard before looking at Sam. "But I can't help you. I think you should go now."

Disappointment filled Sam's chest, mostly because she was certain the man was lying. "Mr. Austin—"

"Go," he stated. "Now."

Sam frowned. Pushing him wasn't going to get them anywhere. Maybe if she could find evidence that he was in debt she could get him to talk, but he wasn't going to admit anything without prompting.

"Let's go," Victor whispered.

Nodding slightly, she smiled softly. "Thank you for your time."

She turned to Victor who had the same frown on his face that she was certain was on hers. As soon as they stepped outside and the door closed behind them, she said, "He's lying."

"He owed money," Victor agreed.

"We just have to find out if it was enough to get his wife killed."

"I have no doubt that it was."

Sam frowned as she put her sunglasses over her eyes. "I don't either. And that is going to break Holly's heart all over again."

They climbed into Victor's car, and he pulled from the curb before Sam pulled the file from her bag and started making notes. She'd just noted that they needed to research the files on the loan shark bust for Daniel's name. "What if it was Tracy who owed the money and Daniel really doesn't know? Maybe his downward spiral really is because of the trauma of losing his wife like that."

"It's nice that you want to give him the benefit of the doubt, sweetheart... Sam." He glanced at her with an embarrassed look on his face. "I meant *Sam*."

She chuckled. "It's fine, sweetheart."

He laughed lightly. "It was Daniel. Mark my words. He was in debt, and his wife paid the price."

"And unfortunately, so did Holly."

Silence fell between them for a few moments before Victor said. "I like working with you like this."

"Me too," Sam said after a moment. "This isn't exactly cyber investigating, but I like it. I think I'll be good at this."

"You already are," Victor said.

She flicked her eyes his way, checking to see if there was even a hint of a condescending smile on his lips, but there wasn't. He'd sounded sincere. "Thank you," she said, accepting his compliment instead of doubting it.

VICTOR KNEW THE MOMENT HE CLOSED THE conference room door that he was in trouble. He'd done so without even thinking, but as soon as he latched it, he sensed the temperature in the room change. He'd avoided temptation all day. He'd been good. All. Day.

But alone in the conference room seemed to be too much

for some reason. Sliding up next to Sam, he whispered, "Two minutes."

She glanced at him. "Two minutes?"

"Let's take just two minutes to..." He inhaled. "Remind ourselves what we aren't going to be doing until we're ready."

She giggled as she turned enough to face him. "Two minutes? That's not much time."

"That's the point." Running his fingers through her hair, he smiled, amazed at the depth of his feelings for her. "Enough to ease the ache but not enough to get drunk."

She lifted her brows. "Maybe comparing me to an addiction isn't the best idea since we just left Daniel Austin literally living in the consequences of his inability to get help for his drinking."

"But addiction is the only way I can explain why I can't resist you." Cupping the back of her head, Victor dipped her slightly as he put his mouth on hers. Like the first time they kissed, he slowly seduced her mouth with his, gently prodding with his tongue and tenderly sucking at her lips. Sam was open to his kiss and reacted by wrapping her arms over his shoulders caressing the back of his neck with her fingertips as she pressed her mouth to his, returning his quiet passion.

She moaned when he pulled her even closer, causing her breasts to crush against him before his hand slid down her back to cup her rear, which he again pulled toward him, groaning when she ground her hips to his.

When he stood her upright and broke the kiss, Sam shook her head, brushing her nose against his. "Oh, wow," she sighed as she opened her eyes. "We *so* cannot be trusted without chaperones."

Victor ran a hand over his hair. "Or ice water."

Sam laughed but then her smile faded. She brushed her hand over his cheek. "I've been wanting to ask you something."

"Anything. Wait. *Almost* anything."

"When we were questioning Roger Carlton, you told him your parents were killed when you were younger. Was that true?"

"Yeah," he said softly. Thinking about that time of his life was still hard. The trauma of losing his parents still haunted him and Javier.

"Can I ask..."

Victor sighed. "They tried to start a neighborhood watch. They wanted us and the other kids around us to be safe. Drug runners and gang members don't want to be watched."

Sam closed her eyes. "I'm so sorry."

"Thank you. It was... It was hard, but it shaped us into who we are now. It's why we do what we do."

Sam nodded her understanding. "Thank you for telling me."

"What about you? Why do you do this?"

She shrugged. "I'm just good at hacking into systems. I kind of fell into it. Speaking of which," Sam said, "I've been digging into Jason McDee's past. As much as guys like that can be looked into. Before moving here, he was in Philadelphia. Same kind of work, which is so shocking," she said with flat sarcasm.

"Did he have an arrest record there?"

"Yeah. Pretty much the kind of misdemeanor shit you'd expect from a kid with no solid upbringing. What was more interesting, at least in my mind," she said, opening a folder, "is that the same guy who owns the pay advance shop that Roger owes, owns a few other shops. Including one in Philadelphia."

"Same boss, new city?"

"That's my guess. Maybe they moved him before he got too familiar with the local police."

"Isn't that what Roger said? They swoop in, do the collecting, and then disappear."

Sam nodded. "Which means our guy could be anywhere."

Victor frowned. "Given the amount of time that has gone by since the murders, he might not even be part of their... team? Do we call it a team?"

"Band of thieves," she muttered.

"He could be anywhere."

"I'm still looking into the owner of this company. I'm sure it's no surprise that the records are sketchy at best."

Victor skimmed over her notes. "How do we find out if Daniel Austin owed this guy money?"

Sam rolled her head back and blew out a long breath. "We keep digging."

"Why are you being so dramatic?"

"Because the records I came across are photos of handwritten accounting books."

"They're not digitized?"

"Nope."

"Great," he muttered.

$$[\ 10 \ ]$$

Sitting in her old office at E.I., Sam used her laptop to search old police records. Jason McDee had an interesting life of crime. Sam wasn't sure how he'd avoided prison, but he always seemed to get out of whatever trouble he'd gotten into by settling the case. Sam hadn't found a way to follow those money trails, but she was making notes. A *lot* of notes.

Victor was going through the handwritten ledgers photocopied from the police reports. He would be thrilled—or pissed—when she gave him this latest list of names and numbers to look for line by line since the ledgers weren't digitized. But it had to be done. There was no way Jason had paid off all those court fees and settlements. She was quite certain his boss had been behind that, but she'd yet to find a way to prove it.

She'd yet to find a way to prove anything. But there were crumbs and common sense that led them to one conclusion— Roger Carlton and Dennis Austin were ultimately responsible for the losses of their loved ones. But proof? Sam hadn't found a damn thing in that department.

With a shake of her head, Sam set aside the task of finding needles in the proverbial haystack. Trying to tie Jason McDee to anything worse than assault was like going down a very dark and depressing rabbit hole. There were too many options, too many trails to follow, too many breadcrumbs to pick up.

She needed to focus on finding ties to two things: Roger Carlton and Daniel Austin. The problem was, she didn't know which trails to follow to lead her to those two men. Victor had once told her to throw spaghetti against the wall to see what stuck. However, even that seemed overwhelming at the moment.

Sam was tempted to scream. She was certain if someone else, anyone from HEARTS or E.I., was looking at these files they'd immediately see whatever it was she was missing. Closing her eyes, she took several deep breaths to calm herself and focus.

Jason McDee was the heavy for a loan shark.

Presumably, the man who had killed those women had been the heavy for a loan shark, too.

She knew who the loan shark was. She had the records.

So... How could she find a mystery man for a company that likely didn't keep employee records?

They would have had to have paid him, and they would have had to have kept track of that. Companies like this wanted to know where every penny went. So. There was a record. She just had to find it.

Calm down, Sam, she told herself. *Take a breath and slow down.*

"Okay," she whispered, grabbing a copy of the loan shark's ledger that she'd kept.

She started her search about a month before the date that Tracy Austin had been murdered and moved forward until a few weeks after Annette had been killed.

Sam's eyes were dry and tired, but she read line by line by line until something stood out. The word *Tinman* had been written in the books days before Tracy's murder and again right after Annette's.

That was it. Just *Tinman.*

And each entry had *MISC.* in the description where nearly every other entry had a detailed reason why the money had changed hands. Even deposits had a lengthy explanation.

And then, in the next column, was an extraordinary amount of money. At least for a so-called miscellaneous fee in 1989. There was no reason for these debits. It was almost as if someone didn't want anyone to be able to trace the payee or the reason they were paid.

Almost like...the loan shark paid someone for something they didn't want traced back to them.

"Tinman," Sam whispered.

Just saying that word made something inside her shiver. She closed her eyes and pictured the man Holly had described in her notes. Giving the image that name made him seem so much more malicious than Sam had ever imagined.

She read through several more pages but didn't find the

name again. Roger had told them they'd never find the person responsible for what had happened to his daughter because they brought collectors in from out of town. They'd never trace him.

Bullshit. Sam would find him. She'd spend the rest of her life looking. So would everyone else at HEARTS, and she suspected Victor wouldn't give up so easily either. They'd find the bastard. Wherever he was.

Tapping her acrylic nails on her desk, Sam thought for a while before opening a browser on her computer, she went into the public arrest records and searched for keyword *Tinman.*

Nothing.

She tried *Tin Man.*

Nothing again.

Damn. She figured that would be too easy.

Frustrated, she slammed her fingers into the keys as she opened another window in her browser and visited a site to do a national criminal search. Pecking away, she took out her aggression on the keyboard. She was tired. She was angry. She was ready to wrap this up so Holly could find the peace that had evaded her for so long.

"You break it, you buy it," Victor said coming into the office.

She didn't laugh. She was too irritated with herself for not finding this man faster.

"Sam?" Victor asked cautiously.

Frowning when her search came up empty yet again, she sat back and eyed him. "Have you seen anything referencing *Tinman?*" she asked.

Victor creased his brow. "No. Doesn't sound familiar."

"There were two entries in the ledger for Tinman. Both were miscellaneous fees of well over a hundred thousand dollars. Both were in December 1989. Remember what Roger said? They'd bring someone in from out of town and he'd disappear just as quickly."

Victor nodded. "He did say that."

"I can't find any other payments to this Tinman. Only two. Only in December 1989. That's him, Victor." She put her hand to her chest as the odd feeling filled her again. "I know it. I can feel it. That's the man who broke into their homes and murdered them."

"Tinman," he said softly as if testing the word on his lips. However, he didn't seem nearly as affected by saying it as Sam had.

"I did a search of the local records and didn't find any convicts with that alias tied to their records," she said.

"Did you check national records or just local?"

"I just started a national search. Who the hell knows how many criminals use the alias Tinman, though?"

"Yes, but not all of them will fit the description we have."

He eased down across from her. "Are you okay?"

"Tired," she admitted. "Do you know about the Tin Man?"

"From *Wizard of Oz*?" he asked softly.

She nodded as sadness washed over her. "He didn't have a heart." The tears that filled her eyes surprised her. Blinking rapidly, she tried to force them back, but one escaped, and she had to wipe it away. "Holly saw everything he did to her mother. He was ruthless. Brutal. He raped her and then stabbed her over and over until—"

"I know," Victor said softly. "Maybe you should take a break."

She glanced at him. "No, I can't."

"You can."

"I can't," she stated more firmly. "Not until I find him."

"No one expects you to find him today, Sam. Or even tomorrow. These things take time."

"I know, but..." She licked her lips and blew out a breath as she rubbed her eyes. Finally, she dropped her hand and looked at him. "I feel like I'm failing Holly. I feel like someone else would have solved this by now."

"You've been working on this for days, Sam, not years. Give yourself a break."

"I'm not so good at that," she confessed.

She returned her attention to her screen as picture after picture started to pop up. She dismissed the criminals nicknamed Tinman as quickly as their photos appeared. Until a bald man with thin lips and terrifyingly hollow eyes appeared. She skimmed his description.

Six feet three inches.
Two-hundred seven pounds.
Dagger tattoo on his right forearm.

She actually felt the color drain from her face as her heart nearly stopped beating. Dear God. She felt as if she were looking at a demon trapped in human flesh.

"Oh my God," she said as she widened her eyes. A chill

ran through her, settling in her core. The image on her screen was terrifying. Even though it was only a photo, she'd swear the eyes looking back at her were empty. Like the man had no soul. Something in her screamed out. This was him.

This was the man who had brutalized at least two women in the late eighties. This was the man who had ruined Holly's life. Sam was tempted to grab her phone. She wanted to call Holly but stopped.

Holly had spent so much of her life looking for this man so she could... Whatever she planned to do once she'd found him. But finding this man was going to be devastating too. Holly was strong, but she wasn't made of stone.

And what if Sam was wrong? What if this wasn't him?

"Sam?" Victor asked, breaking her panicked train of thought. He walked around the desk and leaned over her to see what had caused her to freeze. "Whoa."

"It's him," she whispered.

Victor blew out a long breath. "He's in prison. For murder, no less."

"Have you found anything to link this to Daniel?" she asked, her voice trembling.

Victor clicked the button to print a few copies of Tinman's criminal profile. "Not yet, but I'm certain I will."

Sam's stomach twisted. She was certain he would too. "I have to tell Holly."

"Not yet," he said. "We need all the information first. It wouldn't be fair to give her a portion of what we've found without being able to bring it full circle. We're going to do everything we can to solve this before we tell her anything.

Anything less would be like dangling a bone in front of a dog."

He was right. She was so thankful that he'd said that. It wouldn't be fair to give Holly half the story. Not about this.

"You're right," she said.

"I guess we need to get back to it, then."

"Wait," she said after he started for the door.

VICTOR'S HEART ACHED AT THE LOOK IN SAM'S EYES when he turned to face her again. He might not know her well, but the deep lines on her face couldn't hide the truth. The stress of this was getting to her. The closer they came to proving what they both knew—that Tracy Austin had been assaulted and murdered because of her husband's debt—the deeper the lines between Sam's brows grew. The more she frowned. The less often she offered him those dazzling smiles.

She might be frustrated that they hadn't put all the pieces together, but they both knew what they'd learn when they did. Holly's father was to blame for what happened all those years ago. And Sam was going to have to tell her so.

With each passing second, she looked more and more as if she might be sick. Seeing the Tinman, or who they presumed to be the Tinman, had done her in. She seemed to be fraying under the pressure. He reminded himself this was her first real case. Her first time finding the bad guy. And it was pretty damn personal to her. No wonder this was all starting to wear her down. Taking a step closer to her, he opened his arms and gestured for her to come to him.

Standing, she crossed the room and practically fell into him. Though her door was open, and someone could walk in at any moment, he hugged her tight, rocking her gently.

She shivered in his arms, and he held her tighter and kissed her head. He wished he could absorb some of the hell she must be going through. He could only imagine the emotional burden all of this felt like to her.

"That is him, isn't it?" she whispered.

"We can't know for certain yet, but it seems to be."

"I've been so determined to find him, but now... Now it's real. Now I have to tell Holly things she won't want to hear." She blew out a long breath and leaned back, breaking his hold on her. "Her father did this," Sam whispered, and her eyes filled with a sheen of tears that he wished he could take away.

Victor's gut twisted with an unexpected sense of guilt. He wished he had considered what this must be doing to her before he'd acted like such an asshole. She'd been burying this on her own since he'd announced he was looking into Annette's murder. Though it had only been a week or so, he could see how much it had been weighing on her.

Add to that, his behavior and her fight with Holly. She must have felt like she'd been put through an emotional gauntlet. His heart grew even more heavy.

"I'm sorry," he blurted out.

"It can't be helped. Can it?"

"No," Victor said hesitantly when she clearly didn't understand what he was apologizing for. "I mean...I'm sorry.

For everything. For...not treating you with more respect when you started. For finding a reason to fire you because I didn't know how to handle this overwhelming attraction that I have for you. And I'm incredibly sorry that you're going to have to tell Holly some horrific truths."

Sam smiled softly but it didn't light her eyes like her smiles usually did. "Thank you."

Victor sighed dramatically, hoping to get a more sincere reaction from her. "Thank you?"

She eyed him. "Um...thank you very much?"

"I'm here. Begging for your forgiveness. And all I get in return is thank you?"

Chuckling, Sam lifted a brow as she stared at him. "This is what you call begging?"

"What would you have me do? Drop to my knees right here? Prove how sorry I am?"

When he smiled broadly and wriggled his brows suggestively, she blushed and shook her head.

"I am not answering that," she stated.

"Tell me what you want. I'll do whatever it takes to prove my repentance."

She laughed lightly. "I'm fairly certain that you don't repent your previous sexual harassment with more sexual harassment."

"It's only harassment if it isn't reciprocated."

"True," she said lightly.

Reaching out, Victor put his arm over her shoulder and pulled her to his chest, enveloping her in a big bear hug, sighing with contentment when she clung to him. "I'm teasing you," he said.

"I know."

"I miss your smile," he confessed. "I don't like seeing you hurting so much." Inhaling her scent as he rested his cheek on her head, he closed his eyes. "I've made a lot of mistakes since meeting you, Sam. You turn me upside down and inside out and I lose my head when you're around."

"I'm sorry," she said, her voice muffled by his chest as he continued to hold her. "I didn't mean to have such a powerful impact on you."

He laughed. "It's just been a long time since I've had to deal with so much estrogen."

Gasping as she leaned back, she smiled when he laughed again, this time more heartily. "Well, you better get used to it," she stated. "I'm thinking about sticking around for a while."

Victor's heart flipped in his chest at her declaration even though she had used a teasing voice. "Just thinking about it? What do I have to do to convince you?"

Again, her cheeks blushed, and she batted her eyes at him before saying in a sweet voice that he hadn't heard since they'd been intimate, "Take me on a date, Victor. A real date. With the intent of us getting to know each other better. Not that I'm opposed to other things, but I want to get to know you. The *real* you."

Victor took a deep breath as he searched her bright blue eyes and brushed her soft blonde hair from her face. "I can do that. There's nothing I want more."

He said the words and knew he meant them. He wanted nothing more than to know her. To break through the sarcastic facade that she put on for everyone and get to the heart of her. The part that was so broken and sad for her friend. The part that was so easily bruised. The part that he was just beginning to understand was in there.

The kicker was, he didn't want to wait to do that. He didn't want to waste another moment. "How about now?"

Sam gawked at him. "*Now?* What about the case, Victor?"

"This case isn't going anywhere, sweetheart. We need a break. *You* need a break. You look exhausted."

Stepping back, she gave a wry laugh and shook her head. "Are you kidding me? You want to go on a date right now? When we are so close to pinning this on that..." She gestured toward the computer. "That soulless bastard."

Rather than debate, Victor said, "Steak or Italian?"

Sam took a deep breath, and her posture softened as a smile tugged at her lips. She'd just given in. He actually saw her stop resisting. He loved that about her.

Running his hand over her soft hair, he again said, "Steak or Italian?"

"Italian. And I want to go someplace nice," she warned with a tone that let him know she wasn't messing around. "Don't think for one second that taking me to some cheap drive through on our first date is going to woo me. Just because you've milked the cow doesn't mean you don't have to impress her."

Victor chuckled. He wouldn't have dared compare the night they'd shared to milking a cow, but he was completely amused that she had. "I wouldn't dream of it." Leaning in, he put a light kiss to her lips. Mostly because he couldn't help himself. "Go home," he said in a low voice. "Change into date clothes, and I'll pick you up in an hour."

"One hour?" she asked. "*One* hour?"

"Fifty-nine minutes and some odd seconds now," he corrected. "You want to keep debating this?"

She grinned and shook her head. "No. No more debating. I'll see you in an hour."

As soon as Sam rushed out of the office, Victor ran his hand over his face. Okay. So he had promised to take things slower with her, but he couldn't help himself. He wanted to be with her. Even if that wasn't the most sensible thing to do. He wanted to hear her voice and look into her eyes and feel the warmth radiating from her skin.

"Man," he whispered to himself. "You are so in over your head right now."

After shutting down his laptop and cleaning up the papers and files scattered across his desk, he set the work aside to get back to tomorrow. Sam wasn't the only one who needed a break from the gory case. Besides, he had bigger and better plans for this evening than going over that old ledger yet again.

Walking out into the lobby, he smiled as he heard her heels clicking on the tiles as she headed his way.

Sam sighed, and her smile softened as she met him. "Thank you."

"For?"

"For insisting on dragging me away from the office and getting my mind off this case for a while. You're right. I have to take a break. Obsessing about this isn't going to make it work out any faster or better. I'm still going to have to tell

Holly whatever we discover, whether we discover it today, tomorrow, or next week."

He nodded. "It's tough. Knowing Daniel could have had a role in his wife's death is a lot to deal with."

She blew out a breath. "Holly has lost so much. The idea that I might take her dad away from her..."

"Hey," he said sternly. "You are investigating a case. You are putting together the puzzle. You are not responsible for what the final picture looks like. Get that out of your head," he said firmly. "You can't feel guilty for what you find."

"It's not that. I just... I'm going to have to tell her, and I know it's going to hurt her. More than hurt her," Sam said with frown. "It's going to crush her, Victor."

"I'll go with you. You won't have to tell her this alone."

Sam smiled, grasped his hand, and squeezed it tightly. "I would appreciate that. More than you know. Thank you."

"Would you go away with me after we solve this case?" he asked. The question surprised him as much as it obviously did her. He didn't know where that idea had come from. It had popped into his head and out of his mouth in the same breath. "Just for a long weekend," he clarified for both of them. "A few days to...to do more of this. Get to know each other."

Sam grinned. "That sounds like heaven. I'd love to get away."

"You would?"

"Yeah," she breathed. "I have a feeling I'm going to need some time to recover from this case when it's done."

Victor brushed her hair back and took a deep breath as

he looked into her eyes. "I have no choice but to kiss you right now."

Smiling, she shrugged and said, "Well, who am I to argue with that?"

When their lips tenderly came together, Victor felt like his breath was sucked out of his lungs and the strength out of his muscles.

She moaned and opened her mouth when his tongue darted out, and when the kiss ended, she leaned her head back and took a deep breath.

"You have no idea what I want to do to you," he growled seductively.

"Oh God." She leaned back enough to look at him, the hunger in her eyes only adding to the hunger he felt building deep inside. Shaking her head, Sam let out a heavy sigh. "We better get ready for that date while we still can."

Victor nodded in agreement and led her to the door. As soon as they stepped outside, he pulled her against him and looked down. Damn. Temptation hit him again.

She smiled and pulled back slightly when Victor tried to kiss her again. "Let's go."

"Damn," he breathed as he took her hand. "You realize that you are going to be the death of me, don't you?"

Flashing him a sexy grin, Sam headed for the parking lot. "That's my plan."

They were nearing their cars when he noticed someone moving in the shadows. He pulled Sam to a stop and stepped in front of her. He squinted into the darkness and watched. The shadow rushed off, but as the man walked under a streetlight several yards down the sidewalk, Victor let out his breath.

"That was Daniel Austin," Sam whispered.

"Yeah, it was." His heart started to pound as his instincts told him something was off. Very off. "Forget getting dressed for dinner. I'm following you home, and you're packing a bag. You'll be staying with me tonight."

She looked up at him but didn't argue. Clearly, she was as unsettled as he was.

"Follow me," she instructed as she headed for her car.

A few minutes later, he was in his sedan following her from the E.I. office. He was close enough that he could see her continually lift her head like she was looking in the rear-view mirror. He suspected she was more shaken than he'd realized.

They were several miles from the office when she approached a stop sign going way too fast. He slowed, expecting her to slam on her brakes and skid to a stop. However, Sam kept going despite her brake lights going on and off as if she were pumping the brakes.

"Oh shit," Victor said as realization dawned on him.

Sam's brake lights were flashing, proving that she was pumping the pedal, but she wasn't slowing down. Even when the lights stayed on for several seconds, her speed never altered.

Her brakes were out.

His heart rolled in his chest as he instantly recalled Dennis Austin rushing out of the shadows of the parking garage and down the street. Had that bastard cut her brake lines? Was he so desperate to keep his secret that he'd kill Sam to do it?

"Use your parking brake," Victor said as if Sam could hear him. He glanced ahead of her as she approached yet another intersection. "Use your fucking parking brake, Samantha!"

Sam's car went right through the stop sign, causing an oncoming car to swerve and the driver to honk as the two cars nearly collided. Victor followed right behind her, also running the sign. As soon as he cleared the intersection, he pulled around her and accelerated.

The grinding of her transmission let him know she'd dropped gears in an attempt to slow down. That would work...eventually...but it would take time that he was worried she didn't have. She was closing in on an intersection that was far busier than the two she'd just gone through without stopping. If she got to the next street, she was going to get T-boned.

Once he was in front of her, he lifted his foot off the gas pedal. His entire body lurched forward when Sam's bumper slammed into his. He squeezed the steering wheel, ground his teeth, and held his breath as he put steady pressure on the brake pedal until both cars came to a stop.

"Holy. Fucking. Shit." He took a long, deep breath before putting his car in park and cutting the ignition. After another calming breath, he released his seatbelt and climbed out. "Are you okay?" he asked as Sam climbed from her vehicle.

Her stress-filled eyes were now wide and filled with something completely different—*fear*.

"I couldn't stop."

"I gathered. Are you hurt?"

"No."

"Are you sure?"

Sam nodded. "I'm okay." She looked toward the damage to their bumpers. "Did I cause any damage to your car?"

"Don't worry about that," Victor insisted. "Go get in my car. I'll call Javier and have him get over here."

He pulled her phone from her pocket and dialed his brother's cell. "Sam's brakes went out about a mile from the office," he said the moment Javier answered.

"Wait. What?" Javier asked, clearly stunned.

"She's fine," Victor continued, not wanting to admit how shaken he was himself. "But I need you to get here and take care of this. I think her lines were cut."

"Son of a bitch," Javier muttered. "Let me check the parking lot for brake fluid."

Victor glanced around as he listened to Javier walking through the E.I. office. People had taken notice of the accident, but none of them caught Victor's attention. They all seemed like everyday lookie-loos checking out a fender bender. One man rolled down his window and asked if he needed him to call the police. Victor held the phone from his ear to show him that he had things under control.

"I'm on it. Thanks."

"Where was she parked?" Javier asked.

"Second spot from the parking lot entrance."

A moment later, Javier sighed. "There's fluid here. Not enough that her lines were cut. Maybe she's just had a leak for a while."

"Ask Lorraine to check the parking lot surveillance," Victor suggested. "We saw Daniel Austin out here. See if he was anywhere near her car." He looked around again, but he wasn't seeing the neighborhood where they'd stopped. He was thinking on his feet. "If her car was tampered with, we have to get the police involved in this."

"Let's not get ahead of ourselves. You guys get out of there, and you stay with her while I have someone take a look at the car. Until we know what happened, we can't determine the next logical step."

"Thanks, Jav." He rattled off the intersection where he and Sam had played bumper cars. Walking to the passenger side of his car, he bent and offered her a soft smile. "Hang tight. Help is coming."

She simply nodded and turned her gaze back out the front window. He wanted to comfort her, but he didn't know what the hell he could say. He was too shaken himself. Besides, he needed to inspect his vehicle. He didn't want to climb in and assume they'd be safe. Despite being in his dress clothes, Victor lay on the ground and examined the underside of his car. He looked and looked but didn't see any fluid dripping or see any sign that someone had tampered with his vehicle.

Which was as comforting as it was unsettling. If Daniel cut Sam's lines, that meant he was targeting her. Just her. And Victor suspected that was because she would be the one talking to Holly. Holly would listen to Sam. Or maybe because if something happened to Sam, Daniel thought Holly would be too distracted to worry about something that happened in 1989.

Jesus. Victor hoped as hard as he could that they were wrong and her brakes had simply failed.

Within a few minutes, Javier pulled in behind Sam's car. He let out a low whistle as he walked to where the cars were still touching. "She's lucky you were behind her."

"Yeah," Victor said.

Javier held his hand out and accepted Sam's keys. "I've called a tow truck." He nodded toward the car. "You checked your brakes?"

Victor nodded. "Yeah. I'm good from what I can tell."

"Good. You go take care of her. Let me see what we can find out about her brake lines."

He put his hand on Javier's shoulder and squeezed. "Thank you."

"Are you okay?"

"I will be. Let me know what you find out as soon as you can."

"I will."

"Okay," he said lightly as he climbed back into her car. "Change of plans. You are, in fact, getting food from a drive-through. And then we're going back to my place." He winked. "But not for reasons we've gone to my place before."

Sam wasn't amused. She still looked like a deer in headlights. "Did Daniel try to kill me?" she asked in a weak and terrified voice.

Victor started his car and checked his mirrors before pulling away. "I don't know."

Sam sniffled, and he reached across the car to put his hand over hers. She was trembling, and he wanted to do nothing but hold her, but he wanted to get her somewhere safe first.

"What's your address?" he asked.

She rambled it off but then turned to face him. "What if he's there?"

"Then he's going to be sorry," Victor stated, and he wasn't teasing that time. If he caught Daniel hanging around the shadows outside Sam's place the way he had outside E.I.'s office, he was going to drag that bastard straight to the police station himself.

"You have a gun, right?" Sam asked. "I don't carry a gun. I mean, I know how to use one, but I don't carry one. I should... I should carry one. Rene tells me all the time that I should carry a gun, but I just—"

"Okay," Victor said, squeezing her hand. "Breathe, baby. You have to breathe."

She sniffed. "Should we have stayed at the accident and called the police?"

"No one was hurt. No damage was done."

"But..."

He brought her hand to his lips and kissed the back of it. "But nothing. Javier is going to take care of your car. I'm going to take care of you. The first thing we are going to do is get you enough clothes for you to stay with me for a few days. Then we're going to get some dinner."

She fell silent as he drove. He appreciated the silence. He needed to wrap his head around what had happened as well. He parked outside of her apartment building a few minutes later. He scanned the shadows, looking for any sign that someone might be hiding.

"Stay here," he said. "I'll come around."

"Victor?"

"Yeah?"

She laughed lightly. "Um. You gave Javier my keys."

"Yes." It took a moment, but he closed his eyes and laughed as well. "Shit. I don't suppose you have a spare hiding in a fake rock somewhere?"

She shook her head.

"Okay. Plan B. Let's go get food and head to my place. I'll have Javier bring the house key over later." He tapped out the text before leaving the parking lot of her building. Fifteen minutes later, he parked outside his place and helped her gather the food they'd picked up on the way.

They both looked around, scanning the area, bordering on paranoid before getting out of the car. They rushed inside, and he locked the doors and set the alarm behind them.

"Maybe it wasn't Daniel," she said, pushing her salad around the plastic container. "Maybe we just thought it was him because we're so focused on him now."

"Maybe. Lorraine is going to check the security footage."

"He wouldn't..." She pushed her dinner away. "Would he?"

"I don't know, Sam." He pushed his dinner away as well. Taking her hand as he stood, he pulled her to him. He was still holding her when there was a knock at the door.

"It's me," Javier called out.

Sam sank back at the table, and Victor answered the door.

"How is she?" Javier asked.

"Not good. Did Lorraine find anything?"

"Nothing clear. Conner's going to try to brighten it up."

"How long before you hear on the brake lines?"

"Tomorrow at the earliest." He nodded in the direction of where Sam was sitting. "I'm on it. You just take care of her."

Victor whispered his thanks before Javier left. He put Sam's keys on the table and ran his hand over her hair. "Javier is taking care of everything. What do you say we run you a hot bath?"

It took a few moments before she nodded. Looking up, she gave him a weak smile. "I think I'd like that."

He pulled her to her feet and guided her to the master bath. As she undressed, he filled the tub and swore to himself that he wouldn't let anyone get close enough to hurt her again.

[11]

Sam looked up when Victor walked into her office. He looked stressed, and she didn't think it was because they'd both barely slept a wink the night before. They'd been good. They hadn't so much as kissed goodnight, but she'd been too scared to sleep alone, and temptation had hung in the air like a thundercloud.

She didn't have to ask why. He and the rest of the team at E.I. had been all over the accident and the surveillance footage to see if they could find evidence that her brakes had been cut—and tie it to Daniel Austin so they could hand the evidence over to the police.

Sam hadn't told anyone at HEARTS what had happened. In fact, she hadn't even checked in with them since the accident. She didn't want to tip her hand and have to tell them that she suspected Holly's father had tried to kill her.

"What is it?" Sam asked hesitantly.

He held up the ledger he'd been scouring for the last two

days. It was inevitable, she supposed, that he'd walked into her office to give the bad news sometime.

"You found Daniel," she said.

He nodded.

"Was his debt erased too?"

Victor's eyes grew even more sad before he nodded. "The same day that Roger Carlton's debt magically disappeared."

The knot that formed in Sam's throat nearly choked her. She couldn't swallow it down. Couldn't speak around it. Couldn't even breathe.

"I'm sorry," Victor said.

That was the confirmation they needed. Daniel Austin owed a loan shark, and that loan shark called in a collector who raped and murdered his wife to pay the debt. And eight-year-old Holly had witnessed the entire thing.

"That's the proof we were looking for," Sam said. "What about my brakes?"

"Nothing yet. We're still working on it."

She blew out a long breath. "I suppose that doesn't even matter now. Not compared to what happened to Tracy."

Victor moved into the office. He stepped around her desk and pulled her from her chair right into his arms. "I can tell her if you want."

Sam shook her head. "No. She should hear it from me. I owe it to her. But I'm definitely not ready," Sam said. "I don't know how to tear her world apart."

"You're not," Victor said softly. "Her father did that. You're just exposing the truth. She deserves that."

He was right. Holly had spent years trying to solve this

crime and had made little headway. Sam had to wonder if somewhere deep inside, Holly suspected her father's involvement somehow. Maybe that was why she could solve any other case that came across her desk—any other case but this one.

She'd said she was too close to this case, but maybe the truth was she didn't want to look where she knew she should look. She didn't want to turn over rocks that could prove something she didn't really want to prove. Maybe that's why she'd involved the other HEARTS. Maybe she had hoped one of them would figure it out.

No doubt Sam was the last one she thought would actually find the proof she'd been seeking. And now she had to be the one to say the words. Dread filled her chest as she pulled from Victor and sank back into her chair.

"How do you tell someone that her father is the reason she lost her mother?"

"Let's not decide that right now. Let's take some time to process it ourselves."

She nodded slightly.

"I'll put a file together to take to her."

His offer made her smile gently. "That'd be great, Victor. I know she'll want to see the evidence herself."

He kneeled down and brushed his hair behind her ear. "I would if I were in her shoes."

"Thank you for that."

"It's closing in on five o'clock. Give me about half an hour, and then I'll take you to dinner. We'll give Holly some time to settle in after work, and then we'll go see her. Together."

Sam's heart warmed. She hated what she was going to have to say, but at least she'd have Victor at her side.

"Together sounds perfect."

ONE HOUR AND A DELICIOUS DINNER LATER, SAM couldn't seem to stop laughing as Victor told her some of his juvenile actions growing up in a small town in the Midwest. He might have been exaggerating just a little to keep her laughing. He couldn't help it. He needed to see her smile and hear her laugh. The last few days had been hell on both of them, and they needed this reprieve before even more reality set in on them.

Dinner had been delicious. He'd finally taken her to the little Italian restaurant that he and his family had frequented when they were younger. Because he knew the owners, they'd been led to one of the better tables in the small establishment, even without a reservation.

Their dinner had arrived quickly and with larger servings than either needed. Instead of wine, like he'd usually have, Victor ordered the drink special—Italian sodas—and told her all about how this was the very best thing in the world to him and Javier when they were kids.

Sam had eaten the dinner and sipped the drink, seeming to be perfectly content to let him relive some of his favorite memories. Once again, Victor was surprised by how easy being with her could be. He couldn't recall ever feeling so content, despite knowing the hell she had been going through. This was a nice reprieve, and he was happy to give it to her.

"And that," she said, pointing to his hand. "How did you get that?"

Holding out his hand, he examined the scar that ran across it. "This one I got in high school. I was carving my girlfriend's name in a covered bridge, and the knife slipped."

"You carved someone's name in a bridge?"

"Yeah," he recalled with a sigh. "She broke up with me over it."

Sam's eyes bulged slightly. "She did not!"

Victor nodded, vehemently confirming what he'd shared. "Something about me being a no-good vandal."

Sam's smile spread as she shrugged. "Well, you were a romantic vandal. Did she ever forgive you?"

"Only after I sent her two dozen roses and the worn-down sandpaper I had used to get rid of it."

Sam sank back in her chair as she laughed. "She certainly had you by the you-know-whats."

Grinning, he nodded again. "I thought I was in love. I would have done anything for her. My arm was sore for two weeks. But to this day, you can see the spot that I sanded down to get our names off the bridge. All in the name of love."

"Well, you truly are a romantic, then," Sam said gently as she leaned forward again. She traced her finger over his scar as her smile softened.

"Apparently it didn't matter. She forgave me and then broke up with me a month later. A football player invited her to prom, and she said she couldn't turn that down. I guess I wasn't high enough on the high school food chain for her."

"Aww," Sam cooed with a sympathetic pout. "I'm sorry that she didn't appreciate you more. She didn't know what she was missing."

He set his napkin aside. "Actually, she probably did know. I wasn't this debonair back then."

Once again, laughter erupted from his date. "Debonair?"

Victor's smile grew as he attempted to feign shock. "You disagree."

"I would never." Sam wrapped her hand around his. "Well, her loss is my gain, I suppose. If she had realized how *debonair* you were back then, where would I be now? Although," she added as the waitress set a bill on the table. "I will ask that you don't vandalize anything in my honor."

He held up three fingers in a silent vow before pulling his wallet from his front pocket and dropping some cash on the table. Taking her hand, he walked with her toward the exit. Even though the world around them seemed to be on fire at the moment, this had been the best date he could recall having.

Being with Sam was so easy, so natural. He didn't feel like he had to be on his best behavior and tiptoe around some of his less-charming traits. She'd already seen him misstep, and she'd forgiven him. He could get used to this, and that scared him, but he forced the fears away. He wasn't going to let himself fall into the same pattern that Javier and Conner had warned him about. He wasn't going to try to run her off again.

The way he was feeling about her, and so soon, was terrifying, but he wasn't going to sabotage it again. She may not forgive him if he did.

They were laughing as they walked out of the restaurant. Victor slowed his stride, searching the shadows. Something felt off, but he couldn't imagine that Daniel was hiding in the dark yet again. And at a restaurant where he could be much more easily caught than in the parking lot of E.I. Even so, Victor pulled her along faster, taking long strides. As he opened the passenger door for her, he scanned the area, looking for signs of trouble.

When Sam was secure in the passenger seat, Victor leaned down to look under the car. He used the flashlight on his phone to search for any suspicious puddles beneath his vehicle. He didn't find any. Satisfied that his car hadn't been tampered with, he rushed around and got in behind the wheel.

"Is everything okay?" she asked. The lightness of her voice had faded, and the stress had returned. He hadn't meant to upset her, but he needed to be safe. Until this was over, he was going to take whatever extra steps were needed to make certain Daniel Austin didn't make another attempt at hurting Sam.

Victor nodded as he started the car and offered her a quick smile. "Yeah, everything's great."

She must not have believed him because she looked around the car, peering into the shadows as he'd done. "Something spooked you."

"I think I'm still shaken, that's all."

"Yeah," she said. "This has been a pretty stressful week."

"It certainly was," he said, backing out of his parking spot.

"Do you mind if…" Her words faded. "Would you help me buy a gun? I mean, I know anyone at HEARTS would, but I think I'd like you to. If you don't mind."

Victor took her hand. "Yes. Of course, I'll help you. I want you to start carrying one. If you're going to be investigating crimes, even if it's just cybercrime, you should have protection. We can go to the gun range if you want. You need to be comfortable carrying and using whatever weapon you get."

"It's not that I don't know how to handle a weapon, I just haven't been around guns as much as you guys. I didn't really have a need for one when I was the receptionist at HEARTS. I don't have the comfort level yet. I'll get there."

He glanced in the rear-view mirror, taking note of the truck that had pulled out of the parking lot behind them.

"It's better to not carry, then. You don't want to be uncertain with a firearm."

He turned at the corner. The majority of his attention was on the vehicle behind them now. The uneasy feeling he'd had coming out of the restaurant was now sending up flares and waving red flags. He glanced at the glove box where he'd put his gun when they had climbed into the car at his place. He didn't want it just yet, but he took solace knowing it was close. And loaded.

"This isn't the way to Holly's place," Sam said.

"I know. I'm just being cautious. That's all." He offered her a soft smile as he turned at the next corner as well. He checked the mirror. The truck followed their lead. Damn it.

Even though he was trying to be subtle so he didn't upset her, she noticed his movement and turned to look behind them.

"What's wrong, Victor?"

There was no point in lying to her. She was just as upset as he was about what had happened with her vehicle. Though they had yet to prove her car had been tampered with, let alone prove it had been Daniel, they both had already accepted that to be the truth. Some things didn't need rock-solid evidence. Some things were just common sense.

Not admitting his concern wouldn't make it go away, nor would lying to her in some lame attempt to appease her nervousness make her calm down. She'd already picked up on his agitation.

"I think we're being followed," he said as calmly as he could. Though he couldn't appease her, he wouldn't over-react and cause her more anxiety than she already had.

Sighing, she turned around in her seat and gripped his hand harder. "Great."

He switched lanes and turned without a signal. Keeping an eye behind him, he sighed too. "Yup. We're being followed. Hang on. I'm going to try to lose him."

He sped up and took another turn much too fast. Sam gasped as she held on. The truck stayed close to them—in fact, the truck closed the gap. Victor cursed under his breath. He turned again. He wasn't going to lose this guy, but he definitely needed to get them away from where pedestrians could get hurt or he could cause an accident.

"Call 9-1-1," Victor ordered. "Tell them—"

He didn't get to finish what he was saying. The truck lurched forward and slammed into his bumper.

"Holy shit," Sam said.

"Are you okay?" Victor asked.

"Yeah. You?"

Again, they were rear-ended. However, this time the truck swerved, and Victor didn't have to guess what was going to happen next. He hit the brakes, hoping to stop fast enough to avoid getting sideswiped, but the driver of the truck swerved and deliberately crashed into Victor's front driver's side fender.

"Hang on!" Victor yelled as he lost control of his car.

[12]

Sam squeezed her eyes closed and did her best to brace herself. The force of the collision made it impossible for Victor to control the car, which spun once, twice, and then rolled. Sam cried out in pain as her head slammed into the window when the vehicle came to an abrupt stop. Pain spread from her right temple throughout her head and face. Moaning, she slowly opened her eyes and tried to make sense of what was happening.

Her hair hung in her face, and her arms were dangling over her head. She gasped, trying to catch her breath as she realized they were upside down.

"Victor?" Sam groaned when the overturned car finally stopped rocking. She looked at him, blinking in an attempt to focus. "Victor, we gotta get out of here."

She grew concerned when his only answer was a miserable moan.

"Oh, no," she said, putting her hand to his shoulder. The

gash on his head was bleeding. A lot. Too much. "Can you hear me?"

He moaned again, sounding somewhat more coherent. After another horrible sound coming from him, he mumbled, "Get out of here. Go."

"No, I—"

"Go," he said more forcefully. "Get help."

Though she wanted to argue, she knew he was right. There was no sense in both of them sitting there, waiting to see what was going to happen next. In fact, she didn't have to think too hard about it at all. She was quite certain she knew who the driver of that truck had been and what he had planned.

"Okay," she whispered. "Okay, I'm getting help." Sam braced herself so she wouldn't fall on her face when she unfastened her seat belt. Her landing wasn't graceful, but she managed to not hurt herself more. Glass crunched as Sam made her way out of the vehicle. She winced at the feel of her palms and knees getting scraped as she moved, but she didn't stop until she could pull herself up. Dazed, she braced herself on the overturned vehicle and tried to get her bearings.

Frantically looking around her, she finally spotted the truck that had hit them. And the man climbing from the driver's seat. Daniel Austin looked as rugged as ever as he stepped from his vehicle and surveyed the empty street.

Though there may not be any human witnesses, Sam knew there were cameras hidden in every traffic light and some of the streetlamps. He must not have known this, though, because he seemed satisfied that he wasn't being watched as he rounded the bed of the truck and put his hand on a gun resting in the holster on his waistband.

"Don't do this," she whispered. Not to the man closing in on her, but to the universe—or whatever was causing this situation to go from bad to worse. The hardest part to understand was that this was Holly's dad. That at some point in time, Holly was going to have to find out what he'd done. What he was capable of doing. Even now, with her entire body aching and her mind trying to make sense of what was happening, her heart broke for her friend.

Despite all the differences she and Holly had had over the years, Sam loved her friend, and this was not something she wanted Holly to live with.

"Sam," Victor grunted from inside the car, snapping her out of her desperate train of thought.

She hesitated to take her eyes off Daniel, but then he pulled a gun from his waistband. She dropped behind the car, ignoring the broken bits of safety glass pressing into her skin.

"Victor," she whispered loudly, "he has a gun. He's going to kill us."

"Take this," Victor said. He moved around inside the car, and she noticed him reaching for the glove box. His gun was in there. She'd watched him put it there earlier in the evening.

She leaned over enough to look in when he called her name again. He was holding his gun now, stretching his arm out to her.

"Take it."

She swallowed as she stared at it. Though they'd just had

this conversation, and she'd told him how she'd been trained how to use a gun, how she'd held a gun lots of times, and how she'd even shot at targets before, this was different. This was real. This wasn't a piece of paper that wouldn't feel the bullets going through it. This wasn't a piece of paper that wouldn't shoot back at her.

Sam was scared. She didn't want to hurt Holly's father, but he'd already hurt them, and now he was closing in with a gun in his hands.

"Take it. Protect yourself. Samantha," Victor begged. "Please. Don't let him hurt us."

Hurt *us*.

That was the magic phrase that seemed to snap her out of her panic. This wasn't just about Sam. This was about Victor too. Daniel wouldn't just shoot Sam and walk away. He'd take aim at Victor as well. Victor was already hurt, bleeding. He couldn't protect them. She had to.

Taking his gun, she grunted as she stood. When she did, she found Daniel standing on the other side of the car. The sorrow in his eyes conflicted with the way he had just run them off the damn road.

She actually heard Holly's voice in her head. During all the trainings on protecting herself, Holly would say, "If you have to aim a gun at someone, you have to see them as anything but human. If you see them as human, you'll hesitate."

But this was Holly's dad.

"I'm sorry," Daniel said gently. Sincerely. "I'm so sorry I have to do this, Samantha."

"Mr. Austin," she said weakly.

He slowly lifted the gun. "I can't let you tell Holly what you've learned about my debt."

"Did...did you cut my brake lines?"

Instead of confirming what she'd realized to be true, he said, "If you tell her, she'll go looking for those people. She'll try to make them pay for what they did. You know she will. There will be no way to stop her. And she'll find them too." He smiled slightly. "She's smart like that. Too smart some-times. Because if she finds them, they'll kill her. Do you understand that they'll kill her? I can't let you do that. Not after I've spent all these years keeping her safe from them."

Sam shook her head slowly. "She'll never forgive you for this."

A sad smile touched his lips. "I'd rather her not forgive me for this than find out what really happened to her mom."

"She's not stupid," Sam said. "She'll figure this out. She knows I'm looking into what happened that night and why her mom was targeted. She knows Annette Carlton died because her father owed money to a loan shark. I've already told her all this, Daniel. She'll figure out how all of this ties back to you. And she'll figure out what you've done here tonight."

"Sam," Victor said, sounding like he was in pain. He shifted inside the car, but he didn't come out. He probably couldn't with the way his head had been bleeding. And he was hanging upside down. He was probably on the verge of losing consciousness. She had to do something. She had to do something now.

Daniel lifted the gun higher. "I'm sorry. I really am."

Sam closed her eyes and held her breath as a shot rang

out. When she dared to look, smoke was filtering out the end of Victor's gun. The gun he'd handed her. And blood started to fill Daniel's shirt in a strange flower-shaped pattern.

"Oh no," she whispered when he crumpled to the ground.

Rushing around the wrecked vehicle, she winced as she eased down and checked his pulse.

"He's alive," she called out.

"Take his gun," Victor ordered. "I already called 9-1-1. They're on the way, but...maybe you could try to get me out of here."

Sam did as Victor told her and took the gun from Daniel's hand, careful to only touch the barrel with two fingers in case the police needed to get prints or something. She carefully carried the gun to the car where Victor was still trapped and set both weapons aside. "Maybe I shouldn't move you."

"Move me," he grunted. "Please. This is not a good position to be in. The weight on my chest is making it hard to breathe."

"Brace yourself," she said. "I'll go around and release the belt."

By the time she crawled into the broken passenger window, again ignoring the pain it caused her, she reached in and put her thumb on the button.

"Ready?"

He blew out a breath. "As ready as I can be."

She pressed the button as hard as she could, and the latch finally released. Victor grunted as gravity pulled him down. She backed out of the car and rushed around it, peeking at Daniel as she did. He was still lying on the ground, but his chest was heaving from the breaths he was taking.

Sam hurried back around the car to the passenger side and kicked as much of the broken glass out of the way as she could, and then she knelt down to help Victor scoot out of the car.

Once he was free, he fell onto his back and smiled up at her.

She gently touched his head. "It's not as bad as I feared."

"Head wounds always bleed badly," he said breathlessly. Reaching up, he touched her cheek. "How are you?"

She nodded. "I'm okay. I shot him."

Cupping her cheek, he slowly shook his wounded head. "No, babe. You saved us. There's a difference."

She smiled, appreciating his words, but she didn't know if she believed them. Hearing the sound of approaching sirens, Sam let out a big breath. Help was on the way. Thank goodness.

Victor tried to stop himself from reacting, but every step he took caused his ribs to hurt, and his head throbbed like the bass at a dance club. Putting his hand on his left side where the seat belt had caught him and held him in place for several long minutes, he winced and let out a miserable moan. He was going to need some serious recovery time.

"Broken?" a deep voice asked as Victor hobbled his way into the waiting room.

Victor slowly turned his head to his little brother. "What are you doing here?"

"Seriously?" he asked, shoving his hands in his pockets. "You're in the ER, and you're asking why I'm here? Where the hell else would I be, man?"

"Watching the game with Conner." Victor immediately looked at where Sam had sat answering questions as he'd been taken into the emergency room. "Where's Sam?"

Javier followed the direction he was looking. "Well, instead of watching the game when two members of our team are down," he said sarcastically, "Conner took her to see Holly."

Though disappointed she hadn't waited for him, he understood. "That's smart. If Holly's fiancé hears about the accident and shooting, he might figure out that it was her dad. Sam wanted to tell her. Sam *should* be the one to tell her. She figured this entire mess out."

Javier returned his focus to his brother. "She had already called Jack and gave him a quick summary. He agreed to keep Holly in the dark until Sam could get there to talk to her."

Victor narrowed his eyes, ignoring the ache it caused in his forehead. "How do you know about all that?"

"Because she told me when she called to let me know you were on the way to the hospital after being run off the damn road. Do you think you're the only one who makes calls around here? We actually are capable of keeping each other in the loop without you." He grinned slightly. "Man, even when you're battered and bruised you have a head the size of a damn hot air balloon."

Victor opened his mouth, about to defend himself against the accusation, but he didn't have enough clarity to bicker with his brother yet. His head was throbbing, his chest hurt, and he was worried about Sam.

"They want me to pick up some pain killers at the pharmacy."

"As they should."

Victor smirked and held out the prescription. "I don't have a car anymore. You have to take me."

Chuckling, Javier jerked his head toward the exit. "I guess I can give you a lift. Come on."

Javier helped Victor into the car and gently fastened the seatbelt. "Sorry," he said when Victor hissed once again.

They were on the road before Javier asked, "What happened?"

"I thought Sam told you."

"She gave me the CliffsNotes. I'd like details."

Victor sighed once again, clearly recalling every moment from the time he'd realized they were being followed until the police had arrived.

"Daniel Austin ran us off the road and then pulled a gun on Sam. She took my weapon and fired before he did."

"You were getting too close?"

"We'd figured it out. He was worried that Holly would go after the people responsible for killing her mother and get killed in the process. In his twisted way, he was protecting her."

"Will she see it like that?"

"I don't know her well enough to answer for certain, but from what Sam has said, no. She won't see it that way. And she'll definitely go after anyone she can connect to that loan shark who had her mother killed. I'd like to think this is over now, but I suspect it's just getting started. I think Holly will be hunting down some very bad people in the near future."

Javier was quiet for a few moments. "How is Sam doing?"

Victor looked out the window. "I think she's okay."

"She shot someone. How's she doing with that?"

"She didn't kill him. He'll recover." Victor wasn't sure how he felt about that. He supposed it was a good thing, but he was angry about what Daniel had done. More than angry. He was furious that the man had gone so far to stop them from talking to Holly that he was ready to shoot Sam. Clenching his fists because his jaw hurt too much to tighten, he reminded himself that she was okay. She'd defended herself. She was okay.

"That's still a hell of a thing to go through," Javier said.

Looking at his brother, Victor debated how to answer that. "He was going to kill her, Javier. I couldn't see his face, I couldn't see what was happening, but I could hear his voice. He had justified killing us in his mind, and he was going to start with Sam. He was prepared to end her life right there. It scared the hell out of me. I've heard a lot of tough guys make threats over the years, but that is the first time I've been so convinced that someone was going to go through with it. He had convinced himself that killing us was the only way to protect his daughter. He was going to do it."

Javier glanced at him. "Maybe I should be asking how

you are doing with Sam shooting someone. It seems like you might be struggling a bit more than she seemed to be."

Victor didn't want to relive that fear he'd felt when he'd been so damn helpless and she'd been facing certain death, but it rolled through him like a tidal wave and left him feeling empty inside.

"Honestly, I didn't think she'd be able to do it. I thought he was going to kill her. I was scared. Really scared."

"You underestimated her again."

After a moment, Victor smiled. "Yeah. I guess I did."

"You need to quit doing that," he said. He pulled into the pharmacy. After parking, he looked up at the bright sign. "Sit tight, huh? I'll be a few minutes."

"I'm not going anywhere." Once his brother disappeared inside, Victor took out his phone. He wanted to call Sam and give her words of encouragement, but if she were already at Holly's, he didn't want to take her away from that conversation. Instead, he texted Conner.

You at Holly's yet?

Just got here. Sam's headed in.

Victor again debated a quick call to her, but he needed to let her do this. He'd be there for her when she was done talking to Holly. He'd be there for her when it sank in that she'd fired a gun and shot someone. He'd be there when all this sank in and she realized how close she came to Daniel ending her life. Once all that started to come together in her mind, he figured she'd be a mess.

I've been released from the hospital, Victor texted Conner. *Bring her to my place when you're done.*

Roger that.

Victor put his phone aside and closed his eyes. Things were starting to sink in for him too. Not just the danger he and Sam were in, but that his car had been totaled. His body was battered.

The only thing that didn't seem damaged right now was his heart. His heart was full in a way he hadn't ever expected. And he knew why. It was far too soon to say he was in love with Sam, but he knew it was something worth keeping.

Smiling to himself, he looked up at the stars. The last few weeks had been tough, but things were going to get better now. He had no doubt about that.

[13]

THE LAST TIME Sam was this nervous to talk to Holly was when she'd told her she had been fired from E.I. This was worse, though. So much worse. But she had to do it. Jack had offered, but Sam had learned the truth, and Sam should be the one to tell her. It wasn't fair to force Jack to say the words that Sam could barely process.

Holly's dad had been responsible for her mother's rape and murder. Holly's dad had been responsible for the trauma that had followed her all her life. And Holly's dad had run Sam and Victor off the road and then pulled a weapon on them.

No. Sam couldn't force Jack to say those words. But she was glad he was going to be there for Holly when Sam had to say them. As she approached the house, Sam wished she had called in the rest of the HEARTS. Holly was going to be devastated. But Jack was there. Holly had Jack.

So, the reinforcements, Sam realized, were probably for her.

She was walking up the front steps when Jack opened the door and gave her a weak smile. He winced as she stepped into the house.

"Hell of a bruise you got coming in there. Did you get checked out?"

She nodded. "I'll be okay."

"You sure?" he asked.

"Where is she?"

Just then Holly poked her head from the kitchen with curiosity on her face.

Sam's heart rolled over in her chest, and she almost started to cry. She felt so bad about what she was going to have to tell her friend.

Jack put his hand to the middle of her back in a show of support and gestured for her to walk deeper into the house.

"What the hell happened?" Holly asked as she got a look at Sam's appearance.

Sam looked down at herself. Her jeans were torn from the accident, and blood had seeped through the material at her knees. She was scraped and bruised, but she would be okay.

"Victor and I," she said in a weak and trembling voice. She cleared her throat.

"You want a drink?" Jack asked.

Sam shook her head and drew a deep breath.

Holly gingerly touched Sam's chin and tilted her head to examine the bruise that Jack had noticed.

"Sam? What happened?"

"We were run off the road."

Creasing her brow, Holly searched her eyes. "What?"

"Can we sit?" Sam asked. She laughed softly as she realized it wasn't just her voice that was trembling. Her entire body was shaking.

Holly hovered over her as she led her to a chair and eased her down. Kneeling beside her, she looked at Sam's scraped knee through her torn slacks.

"Where's Victor?"

"He, um, they took him to the ER, but we agreed I should come here. To talk to you."

Holly looked confused for a moment but then her cheeks paled. "You found him?" she whispered.

Sam swallowed hard and blinked her eyes. Holding her breath, she realized that she should have practiced saying these words. She should have rehearsed how she would break this news to her because all of a sudden, she didn't know what to say. She glanced at Jack, and he gave her a slight nod as if to encourage her to spit out what she'd come to say.

After clearing her throat, Sam looked into Holly's worried eyes and gently said, "We found...information. That you should know. About what happened to Annette. And... to your mom. Why they were killed." She knew she was stuttering and rambling, but damn it, there was no clear way to say this.

Jack put his hand on Sam's shoulder and gave it a gentle squeeze. "Hol, do you want—"

Holly lifted her hand in the way she always did to hush people. Like everyone else in the world, Jack stopped talking. Sam would have been amused any other time. Right now? Right now there was nothing amusing about anything that was happening.

Holly's eyes were boring into Sam's, prodding for a truth that she needed to hear. One that she likely knew she didn't want to hear, but one she'd been seeking out for far too long to turn back now.

Tears filled Sam's eyes as she wished she had thought this through more. The HEARTS should be here, beside her, helping her. Helping Holly.

"Just tell me," she said softly.

Sam drew a breath and mustered up the strength to say what she and Victor had discovered. "Annette Carlton's dad owed a lot of money. He had a gambling problem and had taken loans from some really bad people. Loans that he couldn't pay back. His debt got out of control. He said they told him if he didn't pay up, bad things could happen to the people he cared about."

"And then his daughter was killed," Holly said.

Sam nodded. "Yeah. She was killed, and within a few days, Roger Carlton's debt was forgiven. Marked as paid," she said with a cracked voice.

Holly blinked several times and swallowed hard. "Did my dad owe money?"

Sam couldn't find her voice.

Holly took a deep, shaky breath. "Sam?" she asked weakly. "Did my dad owe those people money?"

Sam nodded again. "He owed them a lot of money, Holly."

"Was it written off too?"

Hot tears fell down Sam's cheeks. "Yes. It was forgiven two days after your mom was killed."

A choked sob left the woman in front of her as she realized what Sam was saying. Sam bit her lip hard to try to control her emotions. She didn't want to cry for her friend, but her heart was shattering for Holly.

After all these years, Holly was starting to get answers, and the answers were horrific. This hadn't been some random act of violence. This hadn't been some bad luck that put her mom in the wrong place at the wrong time.

That man had come for a reason. And Holly had witnessed so much brutality.

Because of her father's bad choices.

Jack stepped around the chair and lifted Holly to her feet. He wrapped her in his arms as a few garbled sounds left her. He hugged her tight and stroked her hair as Sam sat crying. But true to Holly's strength, she pulled herself together in a matter of minutes and leaned back. She took several cleansing breaths and nodded before muttering that she was okay.

Jack sat her on the couch and eased down next to her. He clutched her hand, watching her face, clearly gauging her reaction.

Holly sighed heavily. "I'm okay."

Sam wiped her face dry and then dragged her hands over her thighs. "I'm sorry, Hol. I wish I hadn't figured this out. I wish..."

Holly shook her head hard. "No, Sam. I needed to know. This isn't your fault. None of this is your fault. Please don't blame yourself. I...I needed to know." Her voice cracked. "I needed to know why. Maybe somewhere deep down, I always did know it was something like this. Maybe that's why I could never find the answers I needed. Because I didn't really want to know."

Sam had suspected that as well. Holly was brilliant. Had she been looking in the dark corners of this case, like she would have with any other case, she would have dug deeper into her father's secrets. She would have overturned every rock he'd ever touched looking for answers.

The only reason she hadn't was because he was her father. She either thought she didn't have to look into him, or she'd been scared to on some level because she'd known there were secrets there that she wasn't ready to uncover.

Knowing Holly, Sam suspected it had been the latter. She'd been waiting for someone else to uncover them so she didn't have to. Sam understood. She couldn't imagine having to look at her father and question what skeletons he could be hiding.

Sam's hand trembled as she held out the file that she'd compiled on the cases. "I thought you might want to... This is our research. Our notes. Police files. Photos."

Jack accepted the file. Holly looked at it, and her eyes filled with tears again.

After licking her lips nervously, Sam quietly said, "That's, um, that's everything we've found, including what we know about your dad. I don't know if you want to know... Maybe Jack should go through it first."

"Is...he in here?" Holly whispered, looking at Sam.

"The man who we think killed your mom?"

Holly nodded.

Sam flicked her eyes toward Jack, hesitant to answer, but she had come this far. She wasn't going to stop now.

"The man we suspect went by the name Tinman. He's in prison in Pennsylvania. For murder. His records are in there."

Holly swallowed so hard, Sam heard it.

"I don't know if it's him," Sam said quickly. "We had intended to look into him more, but we suspect that's him."

"Is his..." Holly touched the file. "Is his picture in here?"

Sam nodded.

"This is a lot for right now," Jack said gently. "We'll look at it later, okay?"

Rather than taking his advice, Holly took the folder from him. She stared at it as tension filled the room.

"Babe," Jack started, but she lifted the top and pulled out a stack of papers.

Sam and Jack sat in silence as Holly looked through the papers. The tension in the room grew and grew. Finally, Holly gasped at the sight of the photograph. Holding up a piece of paper, Holly stared as tears slipped down her cheeks.

"That's him," she whispered. The paper shook as her hands started to tremble again. "Oh my God, Sam. That's him. You found him." Holly looked up, and she was partly horrified and partly amazed. "You found him," she whispered.

Jack hugged Holly to him as she shook so hard that she could barely hold on to the file.

"I don't—" Holly started. "I don't know what to do with this."

"Maybe you should finish looking at this later," Jack suggested as he and Sam watched her struggle to get her hands around what was being laid out before her. Years of not knowing had finally come to an end, and the answers were unimaginable.

Shaking her head, Holly stood and started to pace in the way she did when she was trying to wrap her head around things. "Why would he... Why would my dad owe that much money?" She walked to the window and looked out at the night. "Because he's an addict," she breathed. Leaning her head forward, she rested her forehead against the glass. "I thought he always drank the money away, but he was gambling too, wasn't he?"

"Yes," Sam said weakly. "He made a lot of money, but he lost even more. According to Roger, once he got indebted to these people, they made sure there was no way out. Once his debt was big enough, they sold it off to people who would send in someone to collect on the debt."

"By killing people."

Sam was quiet for a few moments. "I don't know if he was supposed to... I got the impression that this Tinman was supposed to just rough them up and send a message. I don't think he was supposed to..."

"Rape and murder them," Holly finished quietly.

"I'm sorry," Sam said. "But I think they called in a bad collector, and he went too far. I think that's why the debt was forgiven. They expected to scare your dad into paying them back, not...not get your mom killed."

"But they did get her killed," Holly said and then grew quiet.

"Are you okay?" Jack asked after what seemed to be an eternity.

"All this time," Holly said with a pain in her voice that made Sam want to rush up and hug her. "I've been looking for the man responsible all this time, and it was... It was him. He knew. He knew, and he could have told me."

Frowning, Jack crossed the room, but Holly turned and walked away from him before he could comfort her. Though Sam wasn't responsible for what she'd had to tell her friend, she hated that she was the reason Holly was so obviously hurting right now.

"I'm so sorry," was all Sam could think to say even though she'd likely said it a dozen times since walking into Holly's home.

Shaking her head, Holly turned to look at Jack. "I should have known. I should have figured it out. I should have looked into him."

Jack sighed. "You had no reason to look into your dad, Holly. No reason to suspect he had a hand in what happened."

"But I should have." Holly raked her hand over her hair and faced Sam. "I should have known. Thank you. Thank you for figuring this out."

Sam wanted to smile but she couldn't. "There's...there's more."

The silence from the living room was deafening as Holly swayed slightly. "My God, Sam. What else could there be?"

Jack put his hand on Holly's back, and Sam drew a breath.

"We caught your dad hanging around outside the E.I. office yesterday. He ran off before we could confront him. But... We haven't been able to prove this, Holly."

"But?" she asked.

"But the brakes went out on my car soon after that. And then, tonight…"

Something like realization filled Holly's eyes as she slowly skimmed over Sam. "Oh, no." She looked from Sam to Jack and then back again. "Did he hurt you?" she asked so quietly that Sam almost didn't hear her. She shook her head slightly. "Sam, did my dad hurt you?"

"Victor and I were on our way here to tell you what we'd found. Even though we still had a few missing pieces, we agreed it was time to let you know what we'd discovered. Your dad ran us off the road, Holly. He caused Victor to wreck."

Holly put her fingertips to her lips as horror filled her eyes.

"He… He said I was putting you in danger by telling you because you'd keep digging until you found the people responsible, and that you'd… That you'd end up like your mom," she said, finishing with a whisper.

"So he ran you off the road?" Holly asked. She shook her head as if she couldn't understand what she was hearing. Sam didn't blame her. It was almost too much for *her* to comprehend, and she'd been there.

Sam once again flicked her eyes toward Jack, who nodded slightly, encouraging her to continue.

"He, um… He pulled a gun on me, Hol. He was going to shoot me and Victor. I had to defend us."

Holly gasped.

"I shot him. He's going to be okay, but he's… He's in

police custody at the hospital. Once he's cleared to be released, he'll be moved to the county jail."

"This is insane," Holly said as she raked her hands over her hair. "What the hell is happening?" She looked at Jack as if he could help her make sense of this. She blinked several times before seeming to gather her wits. "He tried to kill you to keep his secrets. It wasn't about me, Sam. It was because he didn't want to get caught."

"I know," Sam said. "But... Holly, I think part of it was that he didn't want you looking for these people. He didn't want you to get hurt. He really believed that in some twisted way he was still protecting you."

Crossing the room, Holly leaned down and hugged Sam. "I'm so sorry he did this to you."

Sam leaned up and squeezed Holly. Though she hurt from the accident, she ignored the pain and hugged her friend back. Holly was definitely not a hugger, so Sam wasn't going to miss out on this opportunity.

"I'm sorry. I wanted to help you get answers, but I didn't realize I'd have to sit here and tell you such bad news."

"You couldn't have." Holly leaned back and put her hand to Sam's cheek. "I'm sorry he hurt you."

"He hurt you more," Sam whispered.

Holly nodded and blinked back her tears. "Even so, I needed to know the truth. Thank you for telling me." Finally, Holly rose to her feet and slowly picked up the folder again.

"Are you okay?" Jack asked.

Holly seemed to consider his question for several moments before shrugging. "I honestly don't know," she said. "This is a lot to take in. My mom was... She was brutalized right in front of me because he owed someone money? I've spent most of my life dealing with the guilt of not being able to help her, and it was all because he owed someone money?" Looking at Sam, she said, "Did he tell you this? Did he confess?"

Sam nodded and swallowed hard to keep herself together. As much as she wanted to fall apart for her friend, she couldn't keep breaking down. She would cry once again for Holly later, but right now, she had to be strong.

The shock of what she'd said was wearing thin, and Holly was going to start putting it all together in her head. She was going to start seeing truths she'd ignored for years. And she was probably going to start kicking herself for not seeing them sooner.

Holly scoffed as she shrugged her shoulders. "What am I supposed to do with all this? How am I supposed to process this? He's the reason. He's to blame for everything. And he's looked me in the eyes for years, acting like he was as shocked by what happened to her as I've been all my life."

"I don't know," Jack said on a breath as he gently ran his hand over her lower back. "But we don't have to figure that out tonight. We don't have to sort it all out tonight, Holly."

Holly dropped the file back onto the couch and rubbed her eyes for a moment before nodding. "Should I go see him tonight? No," she answered before anyone else could. "I can't go see him. What would I say?" She scoffed but when she looked at Jack, her eyes had filled with uncertainty and overwhelming sadness. "I can't forgive this. I can't pretend I believe he lied for so long to protect me. I can't act like he didn't try to kill Sam and Victor. So what the hell am I supposed to say to him?"

Jack's voice was soft when he said, "We can figure all of that out tomorrow. Or the next day. Or the day after. We don't have to sort it out today, Holly. Take time to let this sink in before trying to figure out the next step. He isn't going anywhere. The police will see to that."

She laughed wryly. "Yeah. He's not getting away with what he did tonight, is he?"

"No," Jack assured her. "He isn't."

Turning to Sam, Holly offered her a weak smile. Sam's breath caught. She could clearly see right through Holly's attempt at being strong. She was shattering inside. Her soul was hurting from what she'd learned, and it was breaking Sam's heart.

Sam had never been the protective one of their group, but in this moment, she realized why Holly and Rene were so fierce in their attempts at keeping their team safe. Sam wanted to stand up and take all the incoming blows for Holly just so she didn't see her friend looking so damn sad. But she couldn't.

This was just the beginning, unfortunately. Holly was going to confront her dad. She was going to learn more ugly truths. And she was probably going to try to find the people who had sent the Tinman to their home that night.

Sam might not be able to protect Holly, but she knew right then that she'd be standing beside her. Helping at every turn. Doing whatever Holly needed her to do to come to terms with what she'd learned about her mother's death.

"Thank you," Holly said with a fractured voice. "Really.

I can't imagine it was easy for you to come here to tell me this, but I needed to know."

"I know." Sam stood and didn't hesitate to hug Holly again. This time wasn't so awkward or filled with tears. Holding her tight, she whispered, "Will you be okay?"

"Of course," Holly said. "I always am."

"Maybe not always," Sam said. "And that's okay, because this is a terrible, terrible thing that you've been through."

Holly sniffled as she leaned back. "Well, at least I have my friends to get me through."

"Yeah, you do." Sam looked at Jack. "Take care of her, okay?"

"Always," he said.

Sam started for the door. She stopped at the doorway and watched Holly gathering the photographs and papers Sam had brought. Jack kissed her head, and she let out another sob. As much as Sam wanted to stay and help Holly cope, that was Jack's place, and she had someone else she needed to check in on.

VICTOR ACHED, BUT HE WAS GOING TO BE OKAY. THE ER doctor had given him a shot for the pain and sent him home. No broken bones or major damage, but he was definitely going to feel like hell the next day. His skin had already turned into a sickening shade of dark purple across his chest where the seatbelt had jerked so hard, he'd been afraid he'd broken several ribs.

Thankfully, that hadn't been the case. He was just banged up. Very banged up.

None of that, he reasoned, compared to what Sam was going through emotionally. She'd been through so much today and was about to go through more. Telling Holly was going to be tough on her, and he wished he could be there with her. If for no other reason than to offer his strength to help her through.

Resting his hand on his abdomen, he debated how badly he wanted to look at his phone. Surely she had texted by now. If not, he could text her. Just to ask how she was doing. How Holly was doing. How Sam was feeling after the accident. Hopefully, she didn't hurt as much as he did.

"Stay in bed," Javier insisted before leaving the room to get him a glass of water.

"I'm fine," Victor called, however, he had to reconsider that as he gave in to the urge and reached to the nightstand to get his phone. He sighed when there was still no message from Sam.

Once again, he could only imagine she was going through more pain than he was. He couldn't quite believe she had to tell Holly that her father had been responsible for the horrific death of her mother. That was far worse than the ache settling in his muscles.

The sound of muffled voices drew his attention. He listened, waiting, but Javier didn't announce who had arrived. He was about to ask who was there when Sam walked into the bedroom with the glass of water that his brother had left to fill. She had a slight limp to her step, but other than that and a dark bruise on her forehead, she looked okay. But she'd been crying. He could see that from across the room.

"How's Holly?" he asked.

Her lip trembled as she neared the bed and shook her head. She put the glass on the bedside table but didn't speak as her eyes filled with fresh tears. Opening his arms, he silently beckoned for her to join him. There were no words. Nothing he could say to make this better. All he could do was be there.

She eased onto the bed and rested her head on his chest as he hugged her.

"She's devastated," Sam whispered. "She was as strong as she could be, but she was devastated."

"I'm sorry. I wish I could have been there to help you talk to her."

"Are you okay?" she asked.

"I'm fine. You?"

"I'm okay."

Javier walked in and frowned at the two of them on the bed. "You both need to clean up before...whatever this is."

Sam sighed and Victor frowned.

"Go away," Victor stated. "We can handle it from here."

"Are you sure?" Javier asked, sounding concerned.

"Positive," Victor stated. However, Javier had just closed the front door when Victor wondered what he'd done. "Damn. I shouldn't have sent him away. I need a hot bath before I can't move."

Sam winced as she sat up. "I'm better suited for that than your brother."

"Well, for certain parts, I don't doubt," Victor said, "but

I'm getting pretty stiff. I'm not sure I can get up without help."

"I can help with that too," Sam said. She grunted as she rolled off the bed. Moments later, she was standing over him, hands stretched out to him. "Come on. Let's do this so we can get some rest."

She pulled him to his feet, and he shuffled beside her toward the bathroom. As she started the water to fill the over-sized tub, he looked in the mirror. His face wasn't bruised like hers, but his shoulder was showing some ugly color where the seatbelt held him tight. His ribs hurt too. He wasn't sure what that was from, but clearly, he'd taken a blow to his side.

He watched as she poured salts into the bath to help work the kinks out of their muscles. And he did mean *their*. She needed to take time to relax too. As hard as the day had been for him, he knew the emotional toll she'd been through was much worse.

Once she stood and put the bottle of salts aside, he pulled her to him and searched her eyes. "Are you really okay?"

She nodded. "I just felt so bad for Holly. But she's strong. She'll be okay."

"It's a hell of a thing to process."

Sam nodded. She gingerly touched his shoulder. "How is your pain level?"

"Tolerable thanks to a rather large shot in the ass at the ER."

She giggled. "Sorry I missed it."

Victor smiled as she brushed her hair back and he got a better look at her forehead. He still couldn't believe what they'd been through. Not just getting run off the road, but everything that had led to this relationship. If he thought about it too much, he had to wonder if he'd gone completely insane. Sam could make him so crazy, but then she would turn around and do something so wonderful that her flaws seemed insignificant. At least until she did something else to infuriate him.

It was a pattern he suspected he was going to have to get used to. And he'd do so gladly.

"Let's get you out of these clothes," he said.

He released the buttons on her blouse and eased it down, looking for any other signs of injury. Her elbow was scraped. Probably from where she'd crawled from the car. He'd guess that was what had happened to her knee too.

"The salt is going to sting these scrapes," he told her.

"I know, but I'll survive."

"No doubt," he said gently. "You're tougher than you look."

Sam giggled lightly as he caressed her cheek. "I get that a lot."

"You're sexy too. Do you get that a lot?"

Sam chuckled as she stepped back. "All the time." She released the button on her torn slacks and, lifting her brows suggestively, let them slide down her legs and pool around her black flats.

"My God," he breathed as his body instantly stood at attention, ready for action.

Sam grinned as she stood there in the black lace bra and matching boy shorts. Even with the scraped and bruised knee, she had amazing legs, and he couldn't wait to feel them wrapped around him again.

"Are you just going to stand there?" she asked after a moment.

"I want to remember this," he said, staring at her breasts.

"Oh, you're going to remember," she said in a sultry voice.

Victor let out a quiet laugh. He didn't doubt that for a moment. Walking to her, he put his mouth over hers as he dipped down and slid his arms around her waist and hugged her close.

"Oh," he moaned against her mouth.

"Hurt?"

"Like hell. You?"

"I'm good."

"Good," he grunted.

She leaned back. "Let go if it hurts."

"Never," he whispered. Sliding his hands to her thighs, he attempted to lift her, but the pain in his ribs made him stop with a hiss.

"Don't be a fool," she whispered. She stepped back and checked the temperature of the water. She glanced over her shoulder at him as she released her bra and let it fall away. Then she did away with her underwear and slowly stepped into the tub. "Come on."

Victor dropped his shorts and moved to the tub. She sat and gestured for him to join her. The water was hot and felt amazing, but his muscles protested the movements as he sat facing her.

"I really want to make love to you tonight," he confessed, "but I'm not sure I can."

She laughed lightly as she grabbed a washrag and dipped it into the water. "Maybe you can let me worry about that."

Sliding closer to him in the tub, she eased her legs around his hips. Though it hurt, he helped her situate until she was on his lap.

"Okay?" she asked.

He hurt. Having her sitting on his lap hurt. Having her arms around him and her chest pressed to his hurt. Even so, he wouldn't dare put an end to their intimate contact. Though having her so close was making his injured body ache, her presence brought peace to his heart, mind, and soul in a way that he couldn't even begin to explain or understand. The idea of putting distance between them was far more painful than his bruised ribs.

So, despite the physical pain, he told the absolute truth when he whispered, "This is perfect. Are you okay?"

"Perfect." Digging her hand in his hair, Sam gently tilted his head back so that she could kiss his mouth. He loved the way she could set him afire just by kissing him. He loved the way her teeth tugged at his lips before she covered them with her own. He loved the way her lips manipulated his into parting so she could dip her tongue in.

Breaking the kiss that had easily taken her from simply turned on to aching with desire, she put her mouth to his neck. Victor ground his teeth and closed his eyes when Sam tilted her hips and took him. Reaching between them, he rubbed his thumb over her clitoris, causing her to jolt.

"Jesus, Victor," she breathed as she rocked.

He loved the sound of his name on her lips. Even when they weren't being intimate. Just hearing her say his name caused his heart to flutter every time. Hugging her closer, he nipped at her neck.

He felt her body already starting to spasm. He thought he was holding on pretty well until she dug her nails into his flesh and started rocking against him. Flipping her onto her back, he took a moment to catch his breath before leaning down and covering her mouth with his. As he did, he slid into her again.

Breaking the kiss, he put his forehead to hers as he started a slower pace than they had begun with. If they'd kept that up, they might as well call it done, because he wasn't going to last long on that road.

She seemed to know this as she embraced the change, easily going from hot sex to making love. Letting his hand slide up her hip, he gently cupped her breast for a moment before brushing her hair from her forehead, causing her to look up at him.

Their eyes locked for several long moments before Victor leaned down to kiss her. He kissed her lips and her cheeks up to her forehead. Finally, he looked into her eyes again and knew he would never do anything that would risk her again. Never. And he would change everything he knew about himself if he had to. He would change the world to keep her with him.

He gently ran his thumb over her lips before kissing them again as his entire body tensed with release. Sweaty and panting, Sam leaned her forehead to his. She laughed breathlessly when he relaxed.

She smiled widely. "That is why I can't stay away from you."

"Multiple orgasms?"

"Incredible multiple orgasms."

He chuckled as he looked at her, but his smile slowly faded as he looked at her flush face. He had come so close to losing her that it made his stomach turn with fear even now.

"What?" she asked hesitantly.

He laughed again, dismissing the plea to never leave him that nearly escaped his lips. "Now that I know your secret, you'll never escape my clutches."

"You keep that up, and I'll never want to." Kissing him one more time, she eased back, and he realized the water was already cooling.

"I'm not sure if I'll be able to get out of this tub," he said.

She grinned. "Good. Then I'll know exactly where you are when I want you again."

Victor laughed lightly. He could certainly think of worse fates than being trapped here waiting for her to make love to him again.

[14]

Though Holly's wedding wasn't the blowout event Sam had been trying to plan, she had to admit the small wedding was perfect for Holly and Jack. Holly had ended up renting an event center and had a corner decorated with a white arch, tall vases of beautiful pink flowers, and a scattering of rose petals to stand on as she and Jack became husband and wife.

A bit of a dark cloud hung over the ceremony. It was no secret that Daniel had been uninvited. Not everyone knew why, but given the turbulent history between father and daughter, Sam had overheard more than one theory. While she cut harsh glances at those daring to gossip at Holly's wedding, she hadn't shared the truth.

The truth was still too horrific for her to get her mind around.

Holly had a lot of healing to do. A lot of truth to resign herself to.

Even so, she looked absolutely stunning as she stood at

the arch in an ankle-length white dress and became Mrs. Jack Tarek. Sam felt a humbling sense of honor to be there, knowing how close she'd come to losing Holly's friendship just a few short months ago.

Much like with Roger Carlton, Daniel would never pay for what happened to his family because of his debts. There would never be complete justice for what happened. He was ultimately responsible, but he hadn't put out a hit. He hadn't called in the collector. In the eyes of the law, he'd simply made bad choices. However, Daniel was going to pay for his attempts on Sam and Victor's lives.

And he'd never earn his daughter's forgiveness. Which, according to Holly, he said that would be more punishment than being in jail.

There was no one left to hurt because of that for Annette, but Holly would carry that weight with her forever. She would forever and always know her father was the reason she'd witnessed her mother's brutal murder. And that he'd spent years lying about it.

Holly had told Sam not to worry about that. She'd rather hate her father for what he'd done than spend the rest of her life chasing her tail.

That was such a Holly way to look at this situation.

Skimming the room, Sam spotted the rest of her team. Her sisters. The HEARTS all seemed to be happy. They were all in good relationships with good men. Not that they needed men, as Eva liked to remind them all the time, despite her continued search for bridal gowns even though the planning for Holly's wedding was over and done.

Eva was next. Maybe Alexa now that she was expecting.

This definitely wasn't the last wedding for the women, but it was the last one Sam was going to jump in and try to plan. Lesson learned. She'd leave that to the bride going forward.

"What are you thinking?" Victor asked, coming up to her side.

Sam smiled. "That I'm happy. I'm really happy. I'm happy for Holly and Jack and the life they are about to start. I'm happy that Alexa and Dean are having a baby and that Eva and Josh have bought their first house. And that Rene and Quinn are a happy little family. And that Tika and Wade are finding their footing as a couple." Turning, she moved into his arms. "And that I have you." She planted a kiss on his lips. "I'm very happy that I have you."

"Well, now that the vows have been spoken, and the first dance has been danced, and the cake has been smeared—"

Sam giggled. "Jack will pay for that later."

Victor laughed. "I have no doubt. Now that all that is done. Would you care to escort me home?"

A thrill rolled through Sam. "Still scared to be alone?"

"You have no idea," he said gently and with an unexpected seriousness.

Sam sighed. "Yeah. I'd love to escort you home."

Something about having Sam back in his home warmed Victor's heart in a way he didn't want to think about. He couldn't move beyond the sense that she belonged there with him, and that was terrifying. Not so terrifying that he was going to screw it up again. He wouldn't let that fear grip him again, but it still scared him how strongly he felt for her.

The scariest part was he wasn't sure she felt the same. It was too early to ask. That much, he knew. But he was in this for the long haul, and he suspected she was too.

They'd just stepped inside when he slid her coat off her shoulders and hung it by the door. Turning, he pulled her to him and kissed her lightly.

"You look beautiful," he whispered.

She smiled. "So do you."

He laughed slightly before stroking her hair from her face. "I don't want you to think I only invited you here to get you out of that dress, but..."

"I don't mind nearly as much as you think I should." Reaching behind her, she unzipped the dress, and the pink material pooled around her black heels.

She tilted her head up, beckoning his lips to hers, and moaned when they finally met. Unlike the soft setting of the room, his kiss was hard as his hands ran through her hair, grasping and gently pulling her head until her mouth was positioned where he wanted it. He pushed his tongue into her mouth, memorizing her taste, then withdrawing and moving to her neck.

Sam dug her fingers into his back, and he thanked the universe for this small piece of perfection he had in his life. Her back arched when he gripped the clasp on her strapless bra. He had to maneuver the thing for a moment, but soon the cream satin too was on the floor, carelessly discarded with her dress.

She purred like a lioness as his mouth moved lower,

worshiping one breast then the other before finding her stomach and moving lower still. Victor smiled slightly, sensing her anticipation as he dragged a rough cheek along her thigh.

He closed his eyes and inhaled slowly before kissing his way up her leg until he found the spot they both longed for him to taste. Working his magic on her, it took but a few moments for her to climb the peak and fall off the other side. Proud of his success, he slowly made his way to her mouth, kissing her again.

Gripping her thighs, he lifted her so she could wrap her legs around his waist. He carried her up the stairs to his bedroom, eased her down, and stretched out beside her. When her eyes opened and looked into his, he shuddered. The desire in them was almost frightening, overwhelming him until her lips pressed against his.

Her tongue toyed with his before she ended the kiss and leaned back to smile at him. A wicked smile that made him swallow hard—partly out of excitement, partly out of fear for the sweet torture she was about to impart on him.

Calling her name as he exhaled, he let his eyes slide closed, and his senses filled with the sensations she was creating as she moved down his body, using her hands and mouth to find her way. He inhaled sharply at the feel of her warm mouth taking him, her tongue teasing the tip of him. Knowing his sounds, his movements, Sam stopped before it was too late and slithered up his body, grinning when he finally opened his eyes to her.

"You're gonna kill me one of these days."

"But what a way to go," she teased.

"What a way indeed," he sighed as he wrapped his arms around her and rolled on top of her body.

Sam gasped as he entered her with a quick thrust, her eyelids fluttered but never closed, locked on his as he slowly slid out, then made his way back in. Entwining her legs with his, she leaned up and kissed him, gently tugging at his lip before dropping her head back to the pillow.

Victor smiled as he felt himself drowning in her eyes. He wondered if she could possibly know how much he cared for her, what she meant to him, and if he could ever express it properly. To say he would die for her wouldn't even begin to cover the depth of his feelings.

Putting his hand to her cheek, he smiled slightly before nestling his forehead against hers. When she tilted her chin up, he leaned down, meeting her lips, tasting the sweetness of her love as the tip of her tongue teased his lip.

She closed her eyes and pulled him closer, and he wanted to pull her inside him so he could take her with him, always there, always safe, and never lonely.

"We're not going to mess this up again. I won't let us," he promised as he leaned back, his hands pushing her hair from her face.

"I won't either," she whispered.

Smiling, she kissed him, starting softly but quickly intensifying, letting her moans be caught by his as he started moving faster. No longer able to hold back what he wanted to give her, Victor leaned back and forced her eyes to lock with his as they exploded together, united in a bond that grew stronger and deeper every moment of every day.

Collapsing beside her, breathless, he pulled her against him.

"Victor," she said with a hint of hesitation in her voice.

His heart dropped. Had they not just vowed to not mess things up again? Why did it sound like she was about to test that already? "Yeah?"

"I don't know if you want to work together on another case so soon, but..."

"What?" Leaning up, he looked down at her.

"Alexa's sister has been missing for a long time. She just disappeared out of nowhere. I want to try to find her."

Relief filled him, and he nearly laughed. He probably would have if it weren't for the fact that her friend's sister was missing. Brushing hair from her forehead, he kissed her lightly there.

"Okay. Let's find Alexa's sister. You can send me the file—"

"Oh," she said with a dismissive wave, "I already added it to your active caseload."

"You..." Creasing his brow, he said. "Wait. How did you do that? I restricted your access after you went back to HEARTS."

Sam grinned. "Oh, honey, don't ask how I do things. I'm gonna go grab your laptop."

"Did you find a way to hack into E.I. files? Samantha?" he called as she darted from the bed. Her only reply was a giggle. Victor fell back on the bed and couldn't help but smile.

He was going to have his hands full with her, and he wouldn't have it any other way.

Seducing Kate

A Life Without Water

ABOUT THE AUTHOR

As a teen, Marci Bolden skipped over young adult books and jumped right into reading romance novels. She never left.

Marci lives in the Midwest with her husband, kiddos, and numerous rescue pets. If she had an ounce of willpower, Marci would embrace healthy living, but until cupcakes and wine are no longer available at the local market, she will appease her guilt by reading self-help books and promising to join a gym "soon."

Visit her here:
www.marcibolden.com

 facebook.com/MarciBoldenAuthor

 x.com/BoldenMarci

 instagram.com/marciboldenauthor

www.ingramcontent.com/pod-product-compliance
Lightning Source LLC
Chambersburg PA
CBHW060717190726
48289CB00002B/730